Muddy Grave

A Raleigh Cheramie Mystery

By

Jessica Tastet

This is a work of fiction. All the characters and events portrayed in this novel are fiction.

Muddy Grave

Cover photo by Paula A. Clement

Cover Design by Ashley Comeaux-Foret

ISBN: 1481073621

ISBN-13:9781481073622

DEDICATION

*To my friends, Donna McBroom-Theriot
and Paula A. Clement,
who are always willing to help.*

Also By Jessica Tastet

THE RALEIGH CHERAMIE SERIES

Muddy Bayou

Muddy Grave

Muddy Hearts

Acknowledgments

Though this story takes place in a fictional world, it is a conglomerate of the places of my childhood memories. I consult the people around me continuously to keep the perspective of South Louisiana. I also want to thank those who offered information and help along the way in keeping the facts realistic. I want to thank Jason McBroom for his medical knowledge and BJ Bourg for his legal insight. Any mistakes are my own.

Muddy Grave

One

Raleigh Cheramie was going to freeze to death. The weather in Louisiana had lost its mind. Yesterday she'd been fanning herself with her notepad, but this morning December had arrived all at once, and even the parts that were hidden beneath her clothing felt like ice as she waited in this long line to be suffocated with smoke and deafened with loud music.

Exactly why she was waiting was still beyond her. That's where she had lost her mind along with the weather. Barbeaux Bayou, a typical back bayou town with gas stations as big as its grocery stores, was having a party to end all parties. Anyone who wanted to know what everyone else was doing wrong had been invited to celebrate a new "night spot" as they'd called it in the black and white flyers they'd pasted to everything with windows for the past two weeks.

Her companions had decided that it was a spectacle worth seeing. She didn't think it was one worth freezing over.

Mike's elbow jabbed into her side that was slowly becoming numb and she flinched. Apparently, he'd forgotten once more that she was not one of his tough guy friends. Her girl parts were much softer than his gorgeous tight abs. Since she was technically seeing someone right now, she probably shouldn't be thinking about the chiseled chest that he bared frequently, but it was nice to look at. Not that Max didn't look yummy himself, but she couldn't say she'd seen him bare chested yet. Maybe she needed to distract herself right now before her thoughts snowballed.

She looked up at Mike's boyish face instead as he jerked his blonde haired head toward Sheri and Jeff. Jeff's fingertips rhythmically brushed Sheri's fingers every time he swung them in an attempt to keep warm, and their eyes met that second longer than friendly. Now that was interesting.

Mike chuckled. "Going to be a nice night, Jeff?"

Raleigh returned the jab to Mike's side, but it landed more towards his lower waist with the height difference. When they were thirteen, he'd shot up and her growth had puttered out not too long after. She'd had to look up in that direction ever since. She much preferred when her eyes had looked out over his hair.

Jeff stood a few inches below Mike, and his dark eyes were now crinkling at the corners, glaring their way. "I see you've lost the stalker tonight. Going to be a real nice night for you, too."

Ouch. Apparently, the Jeff and Sheri development was just too new for public mention. That explains why she hadn't noticed anything before tonight. Her instincts weren't dead and that was good to know. She made her living on instincts as a reporter these days for the *Barbeaux Gazette*.

Raleigh shivered again, burrowing further into her jean jacket. She lived in Louisiana with approximately fifteen days of cold a year, and a nice vacation to the tropics during those fifteen days appealed to her. "Why again are we waiting in line at a bar?"

Sheri laughed as her gum smacked against her lips. "Honey, the parking lot is chock-a-block full. We have to see what all the hype is about."

"She's not my stalker." Mike grumbled. "She's just a little lonely and confused right now."

Raleigh patted his arm, though she had to reach up to do so. And for the record, his biceps were as hard as his chest. "Mike," Raleigh looked up at him with the sternest expression she could manage though her bottom lip twitched with a smothered smile. "She showed up at work five times this week, not to mention that strange middle of the night visit two nights ago. That qualifies her as a stalker."

Mike's frown eased some but his shoulders sagged. A smile didn't appear as he bent down his head in concession. Good time, one maybe two dates, Mike had acquired Kayla Duncan as a stalker two weeks ago. With her high cheekbones and blue eyes set in an oval face not to mention that long blonde hair, she was okay. Well maybe more than okay. With all that stalking, and her southern drawl and innocent doe eyes, Raleigh had noticed that she spoke in an octave above normal and laughed at everything that was uttered, funny or not. Mike was right about the lonely part though. His reaction to her arriving at work yesterday morning with breakfast had been out of character even for his laid-back personality. Of course, Kayla had rung his doorbell the night before at two in the morning to use his bathroom. The clingy type was certainly not Mike's type. And this girl was working toward an academy award for psycho clingy.

Raleigh checked out the line. It was just as long behind them as in front.

In terms of appearances to all the other fools waiting in line before and after them, the four of them looked like two cute couples approaching the bar. Mike and Raleigh may be cute, but they were only a couple of lifetime friends. There was that incident in college, but it was never to be spoken about again. Too much tequila and torrential tears over a bad breakup had led to levels of awkwardness that made it painful for everyone near. Jeff and Sheri may be heading toward coupledom, but it was too early to tell or ask. Hmm… if that didn't work out, it may be the end of this group dynamic. Mike and Jeff were good friends, and

Raleigh and Sheri were catching up after Raleigh's long absence from Barbeaux. But if it did, there might be a bridesmaid dress in her future. On that thought, it didn't sound good from any angle you spun it.

Finally, they reached the glass doors of the The Seafood Camp. She'd be able to escape the cold, maybe feel her toes again. She tried not to think about the walk back to Mike's Jeep in this wind. Maybe she could convince him to pick her up at the door when the night was over. Okay, so she was pushing it. A bit much for the non-boyfriend with zero privileges.

Nick nodded them in without so much as an ID check. In Barbeaux he probably knew her birthday and how she'd celebrated. Raleigh's eyes burned as they adjusted to the hazy blue and red lit smoky room as she stumbled after Mike through the crowd. The techno beat vibrated up the heel of her boots into her legs, but Raleigh's teeth were still chattering from the cold. She'd never make it north of the Mississippi. The Camp's grand opening flyers advertised itself as a dance club. Raleigh supposed this is the closest Barbeaux Bayou would get to one of those.

She'd never been in a dance club that had trees in its center with a bar wrapping around one side. A balcony lined the top floor and green vines draped down from the banisters. The outer walls nestled booth seating and there were pirogues leaning against the back wall along with a trawl net draping from the ceiling.

On the other side of the club, there was a band area where a DJ was spinning, and there was certainly dancing. At least that's what a few people looked like they were doing. Some she wasn't so sure about.

As Raleigh's eyes burned and blinked less, the long blonde haired girl gyrating on the bar came into focus. Her belly button, nose, and ear piercings sparkled like tiny light beams in the revolving lights. If Raleigh had all those diamonds, she'd find a better place to show them off. Bar entertainment had not been included on the Grand opening flyer. Her cheeks still burned from her one experience at a strip club. What had she done to endure a repeat performance so soon?

A sideways glance at the blonde's thin round face revealed Winter, a stripper who'd worked the same bar as Raleigh's sister. Among life's small favors, Madison had said good-bye to that lifestyle after her ex-boyfriend had held her hostage for over a week and had tried to kill them when Raleigh had botched the rescue. Madison had the worst taste in men, and Raleigh could speak with experience since hers hadn't been anything to brag about either.

Raleigh's chest ached as she watched the visibly spaced out Winter sway to the music, her eyes fully dilated. Five weeks ago, Raleigh had discovered Winter's best friend Summer dead by what the *Barbeaux Gazette* was told to be a drug overdose. This must be how Winter dealt with the death- get wasted and dance on bars. Raleigh would just as well have drunk tequila and drowned herself with tears. She would never dance on a bar in public without falling and making a fool of herself, and besides her curves looked nothing like Winter's even with Spanx.

Raleigh followed Mike as he dug deeper into the crowd. People were stacked up against each other's back pockets, and there was way too much brushing up against lumpy bodies for Raleigh's tastes. Maybe next time they should wait for the weekend after grand opening to tryout the new bar. She hadn't even known Barbeaux's population was this large.

After attempting to side step a rather entangled, enthusiastic couple, she realized she'd lost the deep blue shirt of Mike. The flashing lights made it difficult to focus on anyone. She pushed up on to her toes, stretching as high as she could, to peer overhead. Stilts would have been more helpful.

She turned back toward the door to look for Sheri and Jeff, and Madison's gyrating semi-bare hips on this side of the bar filled her view.

Raleigh squinted, straining through the smoke and light show to make sure it was her sister under all the heavy eye makeup and plunging neckline. There was some serious push up bra action going on to obtain that cleavage because there was no way Ms. Skinny would normally fill out half that size. Her toned legs went on forever in the short black shorts that just covered her butt cheeks. She looked like the two bit stripper she'd said she didn't want to be again. Were she and Madison even related? Raleigh seriously needed to ask her parents for DNA tests.

She had half a mind to drag her sister out by her hair, but she figured she needed to try a different approach first. She pushed her way through the crowd gathered around the bar, wincing as shoulders rammed against tender parts. She'd have bruises later, but for now reaching Madison would be worth it.

She stopped in front of the bar and glared up at her sister, waiting for Madison to stop waving her arms above her head and look down at her. Her lips were frozen in that beauty pageant smile she'd picked up in that one season she'd stalked the circuit, hoping for some ridiculous crown. It's her eyes that gave her away though. They looked straight ahead, avoiding looking down.

Finally, she relented and Raleigh could hear the exasperation over the vibrating guitar. Madison knew that Raleigh wasn't giving in, just as Raleigh knew that her argument would fall on deaf ears. Raleigh often wondered if it were the six year age difference or the gaping chasm in their personalities that prevented them from ever seeing eye to eye. They shared dark hair and amber eyes with green flecks and that was the sum of it. You'd think they could find at least some tedious bad habit in common.

Madison jumped down much too graceful to have only done it once. Raleigh would be picking herself off the floor or limping away if she'd tried that. Had Madison jumped down from that many bars to make it appear so easy? Baby sister had left innocent behind long ago, she supposed.

"What do you want?" Madison hissed. "I'm working."

Raleigh glared at the green glitter across her eyelids. It was distracting as if she'd landed in Oz, and why did her little sister have to be taller than her? Could she not at least be intimidating to her younger sister? "Let's talk about this outside."

Madison rolled her eyes. The glitter gave it the effect of an eight year old playing dress up. "Fine," she muttered.

Madison's temper didn't stop her from flirting and teasing several men as they made their way toward the door with a glaring red exit sign. *Twenty-three, not sixteen.* Raleigh repeated this mantra to herself. Her sister wasn't a teenager, though she was acting the part. Maybe if she told herself to treat her like a sensible adult, she'd poof into a real one. Not likely.

Raleigh's ears rung in a muffled way as they stepped outside into a quiet night. They had emerged at some back door without even a parking lot. Madison pushed a lone brick to jar the door open. Something told her that this wasn't Madison's first night here, even though it was the grand opening.

"What are you doing, Madison?"

"I'm working, Mom." Madison grumbled, tapping her high-heeled boot, arms closed. Raleigh thought she'd have a husband or at least a steady boyfriend first before she had to deal with a teenager.

"You have a job, and it's not dancing on a bar. A month ago you wanted a fresh start. What happened to that?"

Raleigh sucked in a deep breath. She felt a little dizzy. She must have forgotten to breathe.

Madison's expression was statuesque. "Is that all?"

Heat shot through Raleigh's body. "What do you mean, that's all? You're dancing on a bar again! Isn't that enough?"

Madison flashed the look that let Raleigh know she was being ridiculous, at least in Madison's view. Raleigh had seen it so often lately she was beginning to wonder if Madison had another expression. "I'm not doing anything wrong. I get one hundred fifty dollars cash tonight, and I haven't compromised any morals, have I?"

"Morals..." Raleigh stuttered. "You think dancing on a bar shows morals? Where did Mom and Dad go wrong teaching you right from wrong?"

Madison blurred before her into hazy turquoise and purple lights. She reached out and braced herself against the rough bricks of the building. Her anger had burned through her before, but this was ridiculous. It was just Madison. She should be used to her stupid antics by now.

Madison's hands dropped to her sides and her fists clenched. "Just because I'm not a prude doesn't mean I don't have morals. I'm not naked, am I? I haven't had but one drink, and I'm not high. I'm sorry we can't all please the moral police."

Madison swayed side to side. Raleigh tilted her heavy head watching her sway for a moment. Now why would she do that? It was like a pendulum and quite hypnotic. It seeped in little by little. Madison was standing still, and it was Raleigh who swayed.

At any moment her heavy head was going to fall to one

side and cease the swinging of the pendulum. She stumbled toward the rough, sand textured wall as black spots popped from the blur of lights blending together.

"Raleigh?" Madison's weak voice squeaked from somewhere outside of the fog. While she strained to hang onto Madison's voice, the lights became dull and the bricks almost looked like individuals instead of a large mass. Madison's voice didn't come again though and everything evaporated as she had nothing else to hold onto.

Raleigh sank to her bottom into the deep darkness. It was always like this. A complete disconnect from her body. She'd prefer if she could disconnect and land on an island with a beautiful beach, but no, she had to leave and visit the dying as they left their body. Me'Maw's traiteur ability worked the same, but Me'Maw connected to the living. Raleigh was only able to watch people's last moments before they died. As she saw it, Me'Maw definitely had the better end of the deal.

The black spots spread, and she could no longer see the street lamp. Her head splintered, and she began to feel as though she'd be split in two. She needed to release herself in order to embrace whoever was trying to reach her. Her head felt as if spider cracks were forming through her cranium. She'd need to let go before she had a stroke.

Raleigh sank into the tunnel, feeling a rush of air gush through her.

She stared up at the stars. They sprinkled around her like a tapestry, winking at her. The earth warmed her... and tickled. Small movements from within the Earth crawled across her flesh. The stars blurred together into a white spotlight and then sorted themselves out again.

There was something feminine about the body even though she couldn't see her body, only the stars. In a side view, she could see the weathered gray cypress of an old barn with a rusted tin roof caved in. There was also a deep putrid smell of cow.

Raleigh shuddered as she yanked herself out of the dead girl, and planted herself firmly back in her body slumped against the building. It couldn't have lasted but a few seconds, but her body trembled with the switch.

The blurriness cleared, but Mike's face filled her sight. "Are you okay?"

She shuddered again from the residual effect of being in a dead woman's body. This would never be easy, but would she ever be okay seeing the dead? Raleigh would have to vote no on that one.

Two

Raleigh bounced in the passenger seat as the Jeep trundled down the dirt track. She gripped the side bar with her right hand and dialed Max's number on her cell with the other. The Jeep's headlights bounced around the darkened field flashing yellow-green grass while the phone rang two, three, four times.

"Damn," Raleigh jammed the end button.

Mike thumbed his fingers against the steering wheel as he checked out his rearview mirrors. They'd left civilization a few turns back, so unless he was looking for a cow, no one was around. "Are you sure it's out here?"

"I recognized the old Dantin barn, I think." Raleigh paused. It had been so brief, but she'd remembered that old one-way street sign Nate had nailed to the side of it long ago. But the barn had been falling apart then. "I thought it would have fallen down by now."

"Nah, built back when things were built well." Mike bobbed his head. "I was here last week moving bales of hay with Nate."

The seat belt tugged at her shoulder as the bumpy terrain jostled the Jeep up and down. Through the darting headlights, Raleigh caught sight of the old cypress, tin-roof barn. Patches of the tin were missing at the back and the open, front doorway revealed big rolls of hay. Mike pulled the Jeep alongside the barn, and the headlights cast a fuzzy glow around them with the pastures beyond unpenetrated with light.

Raleigh dialed Max's number again and allowed it to ring unanswered. She'd prefer to find dead people with his nice body blocking her view. If she were considering her options, she'd rather be at the bar babysitting Madison. Connecting to the dead didn't mean she wanted to be in the same vicinity as the body. That still creeped her out.

The dead didn't like to be ignored these days though, or so it felt to Raleigh, traiteur to the dead.

Mike looked to her with that waiting, open expression. Cool as a cucumber unless you noticed the fingers he kept flicking against his thigh. He didn't much like the bodies either. "Do we go and look?"

She really needed to find out when friend day was celebrated and buy him an over the top present. Bribery may keep him coming back because her magnet for trouble certainly wouldn't do her any favors.

Go look for a dead body? Raleigh bit down on her lip. She'd rather dance naked. And to be clear, she didn't dance, and she certainly was too modest for naked. "I suppose so."

It wasn't like it was going to pop out of its hiding spot. Lord, she hoped not. She had certainly not volunteered for heart failure.

As the Jeep's door swung open, the biting cold stung her cheeks. They'd had a cold front come in last night, and the temperature had dropped from 80 to 51. She tightened the grip on her jacket, soothing herself with the thought that it would probably be warm again in a few days. In Louisiana, Christmas trees enjoyed the sun. Maybe died with the sun would be a more appropriate description.

Mike grabbed a flashlight from the floorboard, and she walked close enough to feel his heat. The moon hung above them, casting looming shadows around the barn and the trees. The flashlight's clear glow did not reach the darkest corners within the barn. She shuddered. How come she always ended up in these horror movie type situations? She'd much rather a romantic comedy.

Raleigh trucked to the right of the barn with Mike keeping an easy stride at her side. From the vantage point in the connection, they were close. The distance from the barn to the girl hadn't been but thirty feet. She could be wrong, of course. It could be a completely different barn with a rusted one-way sign nailed into its rotten cypress wood. It could happen. She kept wanting to be wrong, to not find a body and have the connection just be a sign that she'd cracked. It would be a relief for that to happen.

The tip of her black boot stepped inches from the opalescent fingers only two inches away and she jerked. She yanked Mike's arm and pulled him back with her.

Mike ran his fingers through his hair as he stepped further away. "Geez, Raleigh."

Raleigh bounced up and down against the chills that ransacked her flesh. She couldn't bring herself to look at the woman's face, but she didn't need to look to picture the wet mud that clung to her hair and the streaks of mud that blotched her moon white face.

Raleigh grumbled. "I told you my wires don't get crossed."

"I know," Mike swore under his breath as he paced. "But hasn't it been enough already? I thought after Summer's death, we'd get a break."

"You try telling them we want a vacation." She'd like to see her greet the connection with, "oh, I'm sorry, I'm on vacation this month, try to die some other day, please." She had a hunch that it wouldn't fly.

Raleigh's shaky fingers jabbed at the buttons on her phone again. On the fifth ring she was hanging up when Max's gruff voice said, "Yeah."

Raleigh's insides warmed. She'd like to bottle his voice and sell it as instant calmness. It worked every time for her. "Max, I'm out at the old Dantin barn. I need you to come out."

Papers ruffled in the background. "I'm busy with paper

work right now. What's this about?"

Her chest constricted. They'd argued a few days ago. She'd forgotten the topic now, but the dismissal in his voice told her he hadn't. "I'm standing over the body of a dead woman."

Silence. Raleigh studied the stars, holding her breath. Even the stars froze in their sparkling waiting for his response.

Time stretched forward. Finally, she heard the utterance of a swear. "I'll be out there in fifteen minutes. Do not touch anything."

The click echoed in her ear. Damn. Things weren't going so hot in her personal life. Not since her weird ability kept crossing into that personal life.

Mike's eyes met her own, but she glanced away. She wasn't ready for any friendly advice. She already knew what her friends were thinking, and she sure in the hell didn't want it said aloud. It made denial difficult. "How's it going with you two?"

Raleigh shrugged. "Not real sure."

She'd spoken the truth at least. Most of the time they were meeting for coffee at crime scenes instead of dating. And with his recent greeting, the idea that her welcome on this side of the yellow crime tape had worn itself out had occurred to her more than once.

Mike stepped further away from the woman. His inability to stay still revealed his uneasiness, though she'd had no difficulty convincing him to come with her. Not that she would have come out in the middle of the night to a dead body by herself. Chicken is what you could call it, if you like. She hopped from one foot to the other to keep warm, avoiding eye contact with the half buried girl.

She searched that small part of her brain that the dead connected to, the part that was beginning to feel empty on a constant basis. Until the dead filled it, that is. It was empty right now though. It was weird for her to want them there when only a few months ago she'd blocked it all out, but four visitors in two months had opened this gaping chasm there, and Raleigh had to wonder if there would be any room for her own thoughts anymore.

There was a lingering shadow there in the corner, but she wasn't declaring herself and filling it up. Sometimes the person stayed until they were removed from the death site. Maybe she was waiting to be rescued from that shallow hole before she disappeared entirely.

After several minutes Raleigh noticed that even though Mike didn't want to look at the woman, his gaze slid there. He'd peek, then look away quickly and twitch more.

"She's dead, Mike." Raleigh said. "She doesn't care if you look at her."

Mike shook his head. "It's still not right."

Raleigh sighed. What was she going to do if her sidekick jumped off this roller coaster? The dead didn't reach out to watch her running and screaming from them, and she must admit that the desire bolted through her each time one paid her a visit. The urge had paled some with each visitor, but still.... She needed him with her.

Mike stretched, his focus shifted to the sky. "She's been gone awhile."

She pushed herself to look at the woman's face, to really look at it. Its bluish tinge nearly translucent flesh was streaked with mud. Her crystal blue eyes gazed up toward the heavens and made it difficult for Raleigh to focus on her. It was like a doll's glass eyes, unmoving but life like. She shifted down only to notice her delicate lips were open in a crooked kind of way.

She looked at Mike instead, her eyes watered but she noticed that contemplative puzzled expression disturbing his Nordic good looks. He thought he recognized her. She felt it.

Raleigh glanced back toward the woman, searching for what Mike was seeing. If Mike knew her, she knew her too. She must have known about Raleigh to reach out to her. That was how it all worked. Below the tinged-blue flesh were high cheekbones and an oval shaped face. There'd been those blue eyes, and upon closer inspection, the caked mud hid the blond hair.

Raleigh drew in a sharp breath through her teeth. The air whistled. "Holy crap!"

Mike's body jerked back. She'd confirmed his growing suspicion, and the air now tingled with his nervous energy. "I don't think we should be here."

"It's going to be okay." Raleigh focused on breathing. In and out. Her body didn't seem to remember the action. She couldn't pass out. No way she wanted to be in the same hole as the body.

The woman was Kayla Duncan, Mike's stalker. Now that she'd seen beneath the layers of mud, she couldn't not see it.

Mike paced, his pace almost a jog. He couldn't look at Kayla now. Raleigh couldn't look away. "This wasn't a good idea."

"Everything's going to be okay." Her body still wouldn't breathe. A small ball formed in her chest and throbbed. Her calming words wouldn't sink into her own chest.

The trembling began as headlights bounced down the trail. Every muscle in her body readied for flight, even though her head reminded her she couldn't run. She'd probably fall down after fifty feet if she weren't shot at for trying to flee the scene of the crime. It wouldn't add to her plea of innocence for sure.

More headlights bounced toward them. She counted ten beams of light, five cars. Great. Max had brought the cavalry. Raleigh shivered, her teeth chattering. The dead body of Mike's stalker lay only feet away. She'd led the cops to the body. No matter which way she looked at it, and her mind ran in all different directions at the moment, she couldn't see how this night would end with them tucked in their beds at a decent hour.

Five cars came to a stop near Mike's Jeep and doors flew open. One after one, each stony face moved toward them, but she could not find Cousin Joey's face among the uniforms. Max stopped about ten feet away, studied the scene with his hand on hip, creasing his jacket, and walked Raleigh's way followed by a suit she didn't recognize.

Raleigh took a deep breath, waiting on wobbly legs for him to approach her. He didn't look her way as he walked past her and approached the grave instead.

Anger surged in and the warmth of it calmed some of the trembling. The smooth haired suit stepped toward her instead. He'd lifted his look straight from the pages of GQ and his over the top cologne made it difficult to breathe—about five yards away. She wondered whom he was trying to impress. Crime scenes didn't really offer anyone worth impressing.

"I need you to step over there with that officer until we come to talk to you."

Raleigh looked around him to Max. He still didn't look her way, though she knew he'd heard the conversation with the quiet of the night acting as an amplifier.

She looked back toward the fashion model detective. "We didn't touch her body."

"Humph... Until we take your statements, I need to separate you two."

"We knew her." In the dim fogginess of her brain, a voice told her to shut up, but she kept waiting for Max to look at her, and she couldn't register this guy's words.

Mike brushed her arm. "We've never had to separate

before."

"Look," His lips straightened and his cheeks tightened. He now looked constipated. He really shouldn't try that expression. "This is how things are done, and I'm here to ensure that they are done right."

She studied his intense glare and hardened, yet handsome features and had the impression that he didn't like her. The intensity of his dislike radiated off of him. Besides from Max and Cousin Joey, she wasn't on good terms with the Barbeaux police so she shouldn't be surprised. Me'Maw had insisted things would get better after Raleigh caught a murderer for them, but nope, their perspective was that she was lucky and should have stayed out of it. Things changed slowly around here. Paint dried faster.

An officer approached and motioned toward an open patrol car. Raleigh followed but leaned herself against the door instead. There was no way she was getting into the back of that car. The officer escorted Mike to a different car, and he didn't get into the car either.

From her vantage point, after only a slight craning of her neck, she could see Max bent over Kayla. Raleigh hadn't paid too much attention to Kayla before tonight. Mike's dating was more in terms of the bachelor meets survivor. The women were usually voted off for one reason or another after a few dates. As far as Raleigh could tell, he wasn't giving roses to any of them or any kind of lifeline.

Raleigh tried to recall any tidbit about Kayla besides her good looks. Hadn't she been married until recently? There'd been some gossip about it. Raleigh couldn't remember any of it right now as her teeth chattered. Someone would remind her as everyone began gossiping about Raleigh Cheramie finding yet another dead body. She'd probably end up with her own personal interrogation room soon. That would really give the gossipers something to talk about.

Raleigh squinted and tried to see Kayla in the dark with all the officers standing around. Raleigh hadn't felt her besides that shadow earlier. Usually she'd feel them leave once found. There was nothing there as far as she could tell. Strange was never good. Well, in her case, stranger was never good.

"Excuse me." Raleigh cleared her throat. Startled, the officer jerked his face toward her. Raleigh guessed he'd been daydreaming. "Is she really dead?"

His eyebrows furrowed together. "Are you okay, Ma'am?"

Why did everyone insist on calling her Ma'am these days? She wasn't old, and she certainly wasn't her mother. He couldn't be much younger than she was. She scoured his chiseled features yet pudgy body and changed her **mind. He couldn't be more than a teenager. Were they recruiting high school students these days instead of torturing them?**

Raleigh snapped out of her rambling thoughts. She took in his shifting weight from one foot to the other as he watched her. He regarded her as if he might need help keeping her under control. "We didn't check. We just assumed she was dead."

His face drooped into a frown. "She's been dead for at least twenty-four hours."

The scant amount of blood drained from her numb face and her legs trembled again. How was that possible? She'd only connected to her thirty minutes ago. She only connected to the dead as they were dying. She shared their last moments, not a recording of the experience for play back later.

Raleigh looked past the line of officers toward where Max stood hovering over someone who was poking at Kayla. No static. No peep. How could she have died a whole day ago? It didn't make sense.

Raleigh closed her eyes to the scene and focused on calming her chattering teeth with each breath.

The darkness behind her eyelids grew on her. She stepped inward, and darkness crept into that little part of her open brain. She let it float around a few minutes, waiting. Nothing happened. Her cheeks grew warm as she imagined the officer staring at her. She probably looked ridiculous. A sharp image shot through the darkness, but it was gone just as quickly as it had come. She'd only been able to hang on to the cloudy night sky and the feeling of warmth.

She opened her eyes and shudders racked her body. Teenage officer was right. She'd died here before the cool front had come in last night. What did that mean? Just when she thought she had her genetic mutation figured out, new surprises had to pop up. She wanted an instruction manual; something short and to the point with no surprises thrown her way.

Max turned toward her. For a moment, she thought he looked at her, but then he motioned toward the officer standing to her right, and she became less certain. Maybe she should request a dating manual at the same time. She needed the section about how to act at a homicide crime scene.

Officer young blood opened the car's back door. "I need to bring you to the station for your statement."

She looked toward the Jeep, rooted to her spot. "Can't Mike bring me?"

He shook his head. "Nope, you can't speak before you give your statement."

"So Mike's going to the station, too?"

He bobbed his head as he motioned her forward. "He'll meet us at the station."

Raleigh sighed and sank down onto the frigid leather

seat. Again. She really hated police cars. And the police. And right now, she was furious with the detective who she'd kissed good night on her doorstep a week ago.

Three

Down at the station, Raleigh rocked back and forth in the eggshell blue plastic chair. She'd been waiting for over an hour and her butt and right leg were numb. Didn't they know people watched way too much crime television for this trick to work? They already thought she was crazy, so did they think she'd have a mental breakdown in this room and make some random confession? Hmm... It was quite possible they believed it would work.

The major flaw in their plan was that she didn't know anything. She was pretty agitated with these plain white walls and hard plastic furniture, so she could start making something up. But then she'd only have to stay longer, possibly twenty-five to life. She'd have to change the décor in here first. She could make it a condition of her confession. Naturally, her number one condition would be chocolate, but wait, she'd chosen this week to give it up. She supposed if she would be stuck here, the size of her thighs wouldn't matter much.

In high school, she'd visited this room several times, and she hadn't volunteered information then either. She'd been interrogated for Ross Blanch's murder, which eleven years later she'd finally proven it was self-defense. She'd thought she'd never have to grace the insides of these walls again. Who was she kidding? That was denial talking.

The door swung open and Raleigh scooted forward in her seat. Mr. No Smile, tough man detective was carrying a manila folder that he slapped down onto the table in front of her. He'd watched way too much detective television.

His forehead crinkled even more than earlier when he was separating her and Mike. "I need you to take me through everything that happened tonight."

Raleigh looked at the closed door, waiting for Max to

come through. Shouldn't he have sprung her from here by now? Shouldn't avoiding interrogation be a perk of dating a detective?

"Well hello to you, too," Raleigh grumbled. "I don't believe we've been introduced."

He glared at her from his chair. "I'm Detective William Blanch, and I need to know about tonight's events."

Raleigh studied her chipped fingernail. Blanch? Her mind raced. Was he part of Ross's family? "We found her body, and I called Detective Pyles."

He thumped his fingers on the table. Not the least bit annoying. Right. "So Mike knew exactly where this Dantin property was?"

Blanch appeared to be in his thirties, maybe approaching his forties. He had a few creases in the corners of his dull green eyes, but the rest of his tanned, blonde features seemed untouched by age. She didn't recognize him, and Ross Blanch's family stayed in the Barbeaux spotlight.

"We both knew. Alcee Dantin was friends with my papa, and Mike was friends with Nate Dantin in school."

He thumped his finger against the folder again. "So the two of you are familiar with the property?"

Raleigh studied his unblinking eyes. Being psychic wasn't in her bag of tricks, but she could tell what direction this was heading. "I haven't been there since I was a kid. Where are you going with this? I thought I was giving a statement."

"Just a few questions to clarify some points that's all." He opened the folder, and a page of scribbled notes flapped into view. She couldn't read a word of it, and for that matter wasn't sure anyone could. "When did you discover her dead?"

Raleigh glared at him. She should not have to do this right now. Exhaustion threatened to overcome her, and Max should have been the Prince Charming that rescued her from having to explain all of this, again. "Do you mean when I knew she was dead or when we located the body?"

He glared back at her, and if his eyes were the sun, she'd have received a first-degree sunburn. Her mouth ran faster than her common sense more times than she'd like to think about.

"Are they two separate things?"

A laugh escaped before she could stop herself. How could he not have heard about her? She was the hot gossip topic every time a dead body showed up. "Didn't anyone tell you that I have a connection to the dead?"

His fist clinched on the table and a vein protruded on his forehead. She wondered if Papa had bail money lying around or would she have to wait until the bank opened in the morning. Was being a smart ass a chargeable offense? Raleigh wouldn't think so or she would have been arrested several times.

He slapped the folder shut. "I'm not a superstitious man, which is why I'm interviewing you."

He was thumping his fingers against the table again. Raleigh summoned her strength not to grab his hand and hold it still. "Maybe believing will help you find out what happened to Kayla faster."

"Your version of what happened you mean?" His eyebrows arched, and he shook his head. "I'd rather find out the truth."

"All the same to me," Raleigh shrugged. "Look, I don't know what happened to her. She didn't show me her death, just her body."

"How did you know where her body was?"

His narrowed green eyes burrowed into her. He wasn't going to let up. This could get tricky. She may have to be normal and answer his questions if she wanted to get out of this one. Normal would take work.

Raleigh allowed her shoulder to sag. She'd like to be in bed right now. She'd agreed to go out tonight, why? Oh, right because she'd been stood up last night, again. "I recognized the old barn when I connected to her, but even then we almost stepped on her in the dark."

She'd managed to keep her voice level. Whenever she had to explain her "talent" to a stranger, her thoughts mixed in a weird way, and caused answers she regretted later.

He tapped on the table again. Seriously, could she break his fingers before he realized what she was doing? Nah, she'd probably only hurt herself. "When did you know she was there?"

"When I connected to her outside *The Seafood Camp*, and she showed me the barn."

His knuckles whitened on the fingers that gripped the folder. Raleigh returned his stare, and seconds ticked by as he struggled to keep his cool.

He grunted, then cleared his throat. He studied his thumb thumping on the folder. "Okay, for argument's sake, let's say I was going to believe you..." He cleared his throat again. A pained grimace crossed his face. "Can you connect to her and tell us cause of death?"

Raleigh laughed. She couldn't help herself. Wasn't that always the question? It would make life so much easier. "Sorry," she cleared her own throat. "You mustn't be from Barbeaux Bayou."

His eyebrows rose again, and danger darkened in his eyes. "What does that have to do with it?"

Raleigh figured she had better give him a break before she ended up spending the night in a cell. When people visited the bayou, they should ask for the tour guide. It would save everyone involved trouble. "Look, I'm not psychic. I don't have a party line to the dead that I can pick up at anytime. They come to me."

He tapped a finger in rhythm of a heartbeat on the folder. Raleigh's leg muscles clinched. This is why people snapped. She bet many murders could be explained this way. "So they have to know you?"

"Reputation will do."

He shoved the folder before her to a blank sheet of paper and then retrieved a pen from his shirt pocket. Raleigh sat up straight as he glared at her one last time before standing up. "Write your statement and sign it. You're free to go after that, but don't go far."

He allowed the door to slam behind him. She wasn't making friends with the police. She must have some kind of repellent surrounding her. Raleigh picked up the pen and spilled the sparse details onto the page. She wished she had more than the half page she wrote, but it was the best she could do. Connections didn't typically happen after the bodies were found, and the thought of not filling up that page was unsettling. It felt like quitting a book at the beginning. The nagging voice of her conscience that sounded like Me'Maw warned that the connection had been unusual. It had come twenty-four hours after death, so there was reason to believe this one would be different. Her instincts told her she may get to see more of that book, but that didn't fill her with warm fuzzy feelings either.

After setting the pen down, she stood and waited for the guard to open the door. In the lobby, the station looked empty. Randy Hebert, a strapping seven-foot guy she remembered seeing in her sister's crowd, was bent over his paperwork at the central desk. The only other person visible was an officer guarding a door. Where was Mike? Behind that door? He better not have gone home without her. She directed her quick indignation to finding Max. He could have rescued her long ago.

She spotted his dark hair and wide shoulders behind a glass door. She motioned to him, and he nodded to someone in the room before stepping outside frowning with a creased forehead. Never a good sign with him.

"What's going on here?" She could be angry, too. Max shook his head and his eyes did a quick scan of the station. "Why am I being questioned by a stranger as though I've done something wrong?"

Max put his hand on her shoulder and steered her toward the front glass windows of the station. William Blanch glared at them from behind the front desk, but that only angered Raleigh more and she had to resist the urge to stick her tongue out at him. Now he was going to ruin her relationship as well as her nerves. Somewhere Raleigh knew this was wrong, but the rebellious teenager inside had roared its ugly head.

"Keep your voice down," Max whispered, stepping between the detective and her. This only made Raleigh want to peer around and glare at him more, of course. "Sheriff's orders are that you be questioned by Blanch from now on due to conflict of interest."

Raleigh released a slow deep breath as her heart lurched forward in her chest. Sheriff Breaux. In high school, he'd been the lead detective on her case. He'd made her cry. Twice. The man was the devil. She hoped he hadn't used their case in his election campaign ten years ago. That investigation hadn't gone so well for him, and he held it against her still.

Maybe she'd be better off leaving this one alone. Even she knew when she needed to be a grown up. "Where's Mike?"

Max's expression was blank and his eyes didn't look at her. "I think he's still with the officers at the scene."

Raleigh looked up at the black numbers of the clock

above the desk. Two hours had passed since they'd left the bar for the station. What was he doing at the scene still? Exhaustion clouded her brain, and she couldn't figure out why it all felt wrong to her. She needed sleep so she could think.

"Can you give me a ride home?"

Max scanned the station again before running his hand over his chin stubble. From the shadow on his face, she could tell it had been a long day for him. "Raleigh, I'm in the middle of an investigation, and I'm waiting for a call. It won't look good if I leave."

Raleigh studied him. Frustration swelled and her throat constricted. The normal electricity that always tingled through her was still there, but damn the man could make her crazy.

"So I'm supposed to stay here until they bring Mike back?" Raleigh noticed his averted gaze, a sure sign he was uncomfortable. He never avoided her even when he'd forgotten a date, so she deduced that he was hiding something from her. But what? "Can you at least find out when he'll be back?"

At that moment, the glass door to the outside swung open and beeped. A few rowdy uniforms strolled through the door, Cousin Joey being among them.

Max nodded in greeting to them. "Can one of you bring Ms. Cheramie home?"

Cousin Joey smiled her way. "I'll do it, sir. I'm going that direction anyway."

At least one officer liked her tonight. Raleigh avoided looking at Max as she followed Cousin Joey out the door. She'd deal with Max later, away from the station. Something was going on, and she needed to know what it was.

"Thanks, Joey," Raleigh said as they reached his patrol car.

She slid into the passenger side of his car without waiting for an invitation; her limit was one ride in the cage per night.

He started the car without a word. Joey had always been quiet and had always imagined himself a superhero. He hadn't changed much since he was twelve. Once on the road, he grinned as he glanced her way. "Another fine situation. I suppose you should have gone into law enforcement to make things easier."

"What's going on?" Raleigh said, feeling the frustration throb in her head. It was closing in on 2 AM and all her senses weren't firing anymore. "Max said Sheriff Breaux gave orders about who's to take my statement."

"We were told conflict of interest." Joey sighed. His focus remained on the road. "Max is just trying to do the right thing. People are talking now that you two are dating."

"Talking how?"

"It's not everybody, you see." Joey glanced toward her a moment. Cousin Joey was only two years older, but with much less hair than her. She said a little thanks to whatever genetics controlled that. "People are saying that with you involved he's not giving all the evidence a go."

Raleigh stared into the darkness of the bayou scenery allowing her thoughts to tumble together as the trees blended into dark shadows. She'd found Summer's body; she'd even found Claudia two months ago. There'd also been that old friend of Me'Maw's last month. It wasn't a closet of bodies though. People died every day and she didn't connect to them.

"There's no evidence that I had anything to do with any of them."

Joey grunted. "Old accusations die hard. Max will probably be removed from the case anyway, so don't you worry." His face hardened except for a slight twitch under his eye. "Of course, Max won't like that. He has a reputation, you know, for closing his cases."

Raleigh studied Joey. This was probably the longest conversation they'd had since she was eleven, and he'd explained about Santa Clause to her. He'd said that he'd known since he was seven because he'd believed anyone who snuck into houses in the middle of the night had to be bad so he'd set a trap, caught his dad, and had been in a heap of trouble. There hadn't been too many conversations since. Had caffeine inspired this long-winded explanation? He wasn't the family alcoholic so she didn't think it was anything stronger than coffee.

Joey nodded, giving her a reassuring smile. "Max will come around. He's just not gonna like being taken off the case, you know."

"He shouldn't have to be." Raleigh mumbled. "I haven't done anything wrong."

She could see being blamed for this. Max loved his job. The man talked cases, thought about them, and probably dreamed about them. She on the other hand couldn't get him to remember to show up for a date. How could a relationship work if he resented her? It wouldn't.

Cousin Joey pulled into the driveway of Me'Maw's Acadian house. The steep slope of the roof cast the front porch in shadows, made worse by the overgrown edges wrapping around the raised house. Raleigh took in the old, dim porch light still on, and Paw rocking in his supersize white chair. She'd noticed he'd been getting up during the night the last two weeks, unable to sleep. She didn't like it, but he was another Cheramie man that didn't say much. Her world was filled with men who expected her to read their minds.

Joey nodded his head again and waved out the window to Paw. "Everything will work out, you just watch."

Raleigh swung the door open, thinking yeah, right. This was Raleigh Cheramie's life, not Cinderella's. "Thanks, Joey."

"Night."

Raleigh strolled toward the front porch, studying Paw. He leaned back into his wooden rocker, sipping his favorite beer. He appeared normal except for the dark tinge to his complexion, which could be from not enough sleep. Otherwise, he looked healthy for an eighty-four year old man who walked miles in his garden every day. Me'Maw wouldn't appreciate that beer though. Raleigh had to wonder where he'd stashed them since Me'Maw didn't allow it in the house.

Raleigh grinned, as she noticed his eyes on her. "I promise it's not as bad as it looks."

He finished a long swallow, and looked back at her. "Tell me when it is, Raleigh Lynn. Just tell me when it is."

Raleigh chuckled. Paw believed she attracted trouble like his tomatoes attracted worms. "Coming to bed?"

Paw nodded. "In a minute."

Raleigh hesitated. Why wasn't he sleeping? He went to bed as soon as the sun touched the horizon. She couldn't bring herself to ask though. What if she didn't like the answer? "Well, good night."

Raleigh inched the screen door closed behind her so it wouldn't snap and wake Me'Maw. No use having both of them awake in the night for her to worry about.

Four

Raleigh took a step and her head rolled. It felt like a twenty-pound sack of sweet potatoes hanging from her neck. What the hell? She hadn't had anything to drink last night. She shouldn't have hangovers without the pleasure of having the drink.

She stumbled as the pavement and green bushes blurred into a grayish mess. Her head drooped down and she attempted to focus on the strappy gold heels on her feet.

Okay, time to wake up now.

A shriek from a distance pierced through her, and she jumped in the bed, eyes opening halfway.

She knew she'd been dreaming. There was no way she'd wear those strappy heels in the cold. She might as well hang herself in the butcher's freezer. Her boots were practical, and Raleigh was extremely practical- and modest- when it came to fashion.

She craned her neck to see the red-lit numbers on her alarm clock. 11:00 AM. Raleigh groaned. She really needed to work on some kind of schedule. Her sleep patterns were as erratic as her thoughts on what she was going to do with her life these days. She'd never officially decided to stay in Barbeaux. She just hadn't left. Probably not a topic to dwell on when she was only half awake.

She needed chocolate. Rich chocolate and caramel. To hell with her thighs and her self-control and every other good thought she'd had when she'd wanted to give up chocolate. She rose from the feather cushioned mattress and trudged toward Me'Maw's kitchen half-awake.

Me'Maw's back was turned from her as she hunkered over a big pot stirring at a rhythmic pace. The pungent smell of roux and onions filled the kitchen.

"Morning, sunshine," Me'Maw said continuing to beat her metal spoon against metal pot rhythm. "I hear you had quite an evening last night."

Raleigh crossed to the candy drawer and yanked it open. "Another dead girl," Raleigh grumbled, wondering who had called to gossip this morning. Whoever it was, had probably fished for details, and she hadn't even had time to tell Me'Maw yet. If gossiping were a crime, Barbeaux would have to be turned into a prison. This morning's suspect list could be anyone in town.

"Ah, don't mind folks," Me'Maw turned, smiling. "Small towns need to find their fun, even if it's at the expense of someone's death. So, I suppose this will keep you busy for a while. Any idea how she died?"

At that moment, Mason shrieked into the room with a large gray airplane in a nose-dive position. His dark brown hair stuck out in all different directions and his Thomas the Train pajamas looked a size too small. Her five-year-old nephew was as cute as a button and as loud as an air boat.

A sharp pain pierced through Raleigh's head at his high pitch squawking, and she groaned and dug around in the candy drawer searching for that sacred Twix. Her hands kept turning up empty.

"Aren't there anymore?" she grumbled.

Me'Maw rested the spoon against the pot, her pale pink dressing gown swaying as she turned. "I believe Mason may have had the last one yesterday."

Raleigh scowled at her nephew. She wasn't above resenting his presence when it came to snatching her chocolate. For someone who lived next door with his mom and Raleigh's parents, he spent plenty of time here.

He shrieked one more time as he crashed the plane into the floor. Raleigh jumped as pieces flew across the rough pine floor.

"Where's your mom, Mason?" Raleigh's voice came out sharper than she'd intended. She was not a morning person, and as far as she was concerned, it was still the A.M.

Mason shrugged his shoulders as he snatched his plane pieces from the floor and sprinted into the living room.

Me'Maw poured water into her roux, blending it as she poured. "She had some fancy party to work today for Denise."

Work was a good sign. Work that didn't involve dancing on top of a bar meant she was still trying. Unless this party involved something worse than that. That was ridiculous though. Madison worked for Creative Celebrations, a party planning business in Barbeaux that was considered the best. Maybe Raleigh needed to get a grip and not worry about her so much. Madison was twenty-three years old, but more importantly, Raleigh wasn't her mother. Big sisters offered advice, not rules.

Raleigh scanned the kitchen for a breakfast that involved chocolate, the only thing that made her day start right. The kitchen hadn't changed in the last thirty years or so. The old cabinets were painted white and the white Formica countertops did not offer up any chocolate.

Me'Maw chuckled. "There's a chocolate fudge muffin hidden behind the bread."

Raleigh scrambled behind the bread container for the hidden plastic bag. Hidden meant Me'Maw had made sure there was one for her though she'd waited to mention it. Me'Maw was the only one who didn't try to convince her that chocolate was not a breakfast food group. To Raleigh, chocolate was the only breakfast food group, and Me'Maw's homemade chocolate fudge muffins were just as good, she hesitated to say better than her morning Twix. She'd begun her chocolate breakfast with Me'Maw's famous muffins at six and had never faltered since.

She bit into the smooth, soft chocolate and waited for it to do its magic and wake her up. Her cell phone chimed, ruining the bliss of her head being coated in chocolaty warmth. She glared at it in its position on the counter by the back door. She'd ditched it there last night to avoid anyone waking her up. She should have stuffed it in the sofa cushion instead.

Raleigh snatched it up mid-ring, noticing Denise's all too familiar number glaring on her screen. Denise was Madison's boss, but Raleigh had worked about ten events in the last month for Creative Celebrations. It felt more as if it were her full-time job these days.

"'ello," Raleigh said, chewing another bite of her muffin. She'd hit a pocket of fudge, her favorite part. No one was going to get in the way of her chocolate this morning, not after six days of depravation.

"Raleigh," Denise said and the connection silenced. Denise probably had that far off, spacy look across her alabaster complexion. Denise's creativity didn't roll over into social conversation well, most of the time. But sometimes she could nail it. It was hit or miss. "Ah, yes, the party. Since Madison was sick today, I'm shorthanded."

Again, silence came over the line. Denise was lucky that she was a genius at planning parties. Wait, Madison wasn't at work?

"Would you like me to come out and help?"

A noise vibrated in the phone, and Raleigh would bet that Denise was nodding her head. "If you aren't busy. It's the Ledet's boucherie, and I need someone to get things started while I take care of all the other details."

Raleigh looked over at Me'Maw cleaning green beans in the sink. She believed Madison was at work. So where was she really? "I'll be there shortly."

What better way to spend her Saturday morning?

"Denise need more help with that party?" Me'Maw asked as she placed her green beans on a towel to dry.

Raleigh nibbled on her bottom lip, tasting the chocolate and wondering if she should say something about Madison's lie. Oh hell, they weren't ten years old anymore. Madison was a big girl entitled to her own secrets. Raleigh had a feeling these secrets were going to be one big heap of trouble soon, but it was none of her business. At least not today.

"Yes," Raleigh said. "I'll go help out for a few hours."

Me'Maw nodded, drying her hands on a towel. "Stop and remind Uncle Camille that he's supposed to train you. If you remind him enough, he may actually start."

Raleigh grunted but didn't comment. She went to get dressed instead because there was no use explaining to Me'Maw that Uncle Camille was a jerk. He was supposed to train her in the ways of the traiteur since Me'Maw fully believed in the tradition of passing the skills down from male to female. Uncle Camille would have rather trained the nearest stranger since he believed Raleigh hadn't saved his daughter. Consequently, the only lesson Raleigh had learned so far was that he felt her gift was wasted on her. Me'Maw didn't know about that lesson, of course.

Back in her room, she glanced around and exhaled deeply. The cardboard boxes she'd lived out of for months were still stacked against the walls. Some clothes had been removed from their containers only to be stacked on top of other surfaces. She'd been here nearly two months and her things were still waiting to move somewhere. Raleigh didn't know if that were true because she'd avoided making a decision.

She approached a stack that had toppled over onto the floor, scooped it up by the armful, and dumped it back into an empty box. The boxes wouldn't give her an answer.

Besides, it was easier just not to think about it. She pulled clothing from the top of another box, dressed, and grabbed her cell phone from the bed where she'd tossed it and headed out. Maybe Uncle Camille would be in a better mood today. Yes, and she'd also win the lottery tonight.

A shutter on Uncle Camille's house had fallen and now rested on the ground. His grass met the front porch and the tree in the front yard drooped too far over as if broken. It was a sad, lonely broken sight, just like the man within. He'd lost his daughter seven weeks ago, and the only thing he'd done since then was sit on an old rusted green metal rocker on his front porch. Raleigh zigzagged around the haphazard piles of old cans and jars to knock on his screen door.

She stuck her head into his three-room shotgun house and called out, "Uncle Camille?" She had no intention of walking in on the man in some state of undress, but she also knew that he wasn't going to get up and open the door for her either.

"Your uncle is in here," A strange, deep voice called from the middle room, the bedroom of the house.

Raleigh hesitated. Uncle Camille had company. He never had guests these days. He was so ornery; everyone had stopped dropping by and instead asked family members how he was doing.

Raleigh approached the room, attempting to peer inside before she reached the doorframe. The smell of body odor, urine, and burnt grease had engulfed her as she'd stepped inside, and she managed to breathe without choking, but just barely.

A long dark haired man hovered over Uncle Camille's still form on the bed. Even in the sweltering heat of the house, her uncle was cocooned in an old quilt that Raleigh recognized as one of Me'Maw's patterns. His eyes were closed, and from his steady breathing, Raleigh could tell he was sleeping.

The stranger was putting away herbs in a tan leather satchel.

"Are you a doctor?" Raleigh asked, looking from him to Uncle Camille. Her instincts were on high alert. She'd never seen him before.

From his deep rawhide complexion to his shoulder length dark hair, she assumed he was Native American. Permanent crinkles touched his eyes, and he appeared friendly enough, but you could never tell these days.

"Of sorts," He grinned. "I am a friend of your uncle's. He called me because he had a fever."

Raleigh studied the stranger. There was a soft kindness in his brown eyes, but it could just be the odor stinging his eyes, too. "He has cancer, but he won't go to the doctor."

He bowed his head and the crinkles deepened. "I know. I treat him best I can."

"Are you a traiteur like Me'Maw?"

He laughed a big hearty booming laugh as he stashed the last of the velvet pouches in his bag. "My people have our own traditions and folklore. I believe you know us as medicine men."

Raleigh's cheeks burned. That was stupid of her. Her chocolate must not have kicked in yet this morning. "I'm sorry."

"Doesn't matter," he said, moving toward the doorway where she was still standing.

Raleigh backed up into the front room.

"No matter what makes us special or what we are called, we always face suspicion from others, so we learn not to be so trusting."

Raleigh's neck flushed this time. Had he detected her suspicion? She still wasn't sure of him. Had he felt that?

"What kind of suspicions do you find yourself under?"

"Young people experiment with herbs, and I'm questioned because I use herbs in my practice. I'm sure you know what that feels like."

Raleigh nodded before she could stop herself. Wasn't being questioned for murder just for finding the body the same?

"We will always be misunderstood, I'm afraid," he continued as he picked up a coat from the back of the only chair visible in the room.

"Did Summer experiment with those herbs?" Raleigh asked. She hadn't heard of anyone else dying recently, and rumors abounded that Summer's death would be declared an overdose when her toxicology report came back.

He shrugged. "Well, I will be back to see your uncle tonight."

Raleigh allowed him to leave, but he had a quietness about him and something else that made her uneasy. She couldn't quite identify it though. She felt this need to talk to him again, but when she was prepared and not feeling so jumpy.

Raleigh stood in the center of Uncle Camille's living area among the trash and beaten furniture. The stillness of the house felt like a depressant, so she looked around one more time at the mess of his house and quickly exited, breathing in the fresh air deeply, unable to fill her lungs fast enough.

Now she'd really be running late to the party.

Five

Raleigh puzzled over the diagram in Denise's sketchy lines as she rubbed the smoothness of the scar on her wrist. She'd probably made it much smoother than normal with all the rubbing she did while she thought.

"I think you're right, Leroy," Raleigh said chewing on her bottom lip. "Set up the slides by the fence and tell Wanda to bring the hay bales for the bonfire to the back."

"You got it, Ms. Raleigh," he said, jerking his head down twice in some old-fashion bow. "Those children are getting right anxious, so I'll get to it right away."

He turned and staggered toward the trailer attached to his pickup but stopped after only four feet. "Oh, I was sorry to hear about that young lady last night. Wanda knew her. Said she was a real nice girl."

She cringed before she could hold herself steady. Leroy didn't mean any harm, but she'd endured questions and comments for the last half hour, and her face now burned steadily under the glare of everyone's scrutiny. She may as well have pushed Kayla into the muddy grave herself.

Raleigh nodded and headed back toward the big tent. She pressed Madison on her cell phone and listened to it ring unanswered. She hung up and dialed Mike, but still no answer. She'd attempted calling both three times already and neither of them was making her feel cheerful with their lack of phone manners. She entered the big tent where Denise was ordering around the chair and table people. Big white tables and metal folding chairs were all stacked neatly on carts. That would be great if the boucherie didn't begin in thirty-five minutes. The deliveries had all been late, causing Denise's nerves to be as frazzled as her uncontrollable curls on her head. The Cajun band hadn't even arrived yet, but several guests milled around outside the tent.

Denise had snapped when Raleigh had made the mistake of asking what had happened. Apparently, Madison hadn't called to verify set up times with any of the distributors as their company policy clearly stated. Four hundred people were due to arrive at one o'clock as caterers, musicians, and entertainment scrambled to prepare for their arrival.

Denise spotted her entering the tent, barked one last order to an uninterested teenager, and shuffled through the pages in her stack.

"Children's entertainment area being set up as we speak," Raleigh said, dodging a young teenage-looking boy swinging a chair wildly about. "What's next?"

Denise picked through the pages before pulling one out. "Give this checklist to the caterers. Thank God the roast began at 4:30 this morning and is done."

Raleigh took the list and headed toward the food station without a word. Denise reached rare form under pressure and her normal absent-mindedness transformed into military drill precision. On a previous occasion Raleigh had learned it was better to take orders quietly. The Blouin wedding had been an eye opening experience after everything had gone wrong, including the backdrop collapsing onto the wedding cake and champagne glasses. Denise had cleared Raleigh's doubts about how she'd created and turned this business into the leading one in all the surrounding towns that night.

The food station tent was bristling with activity as white uniform caterers lugged silver serving containers out the back of a black van with red letters announcing Pistachio's Catering. Who named a catering company after a nut? Thelma Ledet had insisted they use a company from out of town that she'd sworn on her mother's pecan pie was the best. They'd arrived forty-five minutes late, and Raleigh doubted Ms. Alma would have ever taken her pies out of the oven even one minute late.

A short man with a double chin was barking orders in a booming voice, and she figured with such a big attitude he must be the guy in charge.

"Excuse me," Raleigh, said, plastering her service smile on. Thankfully, the newspaper didn't require her to be nice all the time. "I'm with Creative Celebrations. I wanted to give you this checklist and see if you needed anything."

The man's frown deepened as he waved his thick hands in the air. "What I needed was less traffic on the road. I needed someone to know what they were doing when they planned for the parking. I needed a better environment for my savory creations. A tent? How am I to keep my food presentable under these conditions? I would not have come if I wasn't asked by Ms. Thelma Ledet for a personal favor."

Raleigh's smile froze in place, though her neck prickled under the strain of holding her words back. She wouldn't be quitting her day job any time soon, because one day she'd get fired for telling someone about their manners.

"Do you have enough tables and coverings?"

He flipped his hand in the air as he crushed the list in the other. "We'll make do, of course. I'd go see what I could do about this disaster of a gathering if I were you."

He scanned the list and didn't look up at her again. She'd been dismissed. Raleigh's jaw clenched. Forget it. Denise could handle this one herself.

Raleigh walked toward the roasting area. She really didn't have any interest in seeing the two pigs roasting on a rotisserie style grill, but her only other job today was the band, and they hadn't decided to show up yet. Rock star late must extend to the local Cajun band now.

"Well, hello Ms. Raleigh," Ben said, pulling off rawhide

gloves. "We are just about done here if you're asking."

"Yes'm," A flannel guy nodded his head in her direction. "I'm working on a batch of cracklings right now. Gonna' have'em all ready when they get here."

He stood over a large black cast iron pot filled with grease. The soft fat of the pig bobbed at the surface as it began to crackle in the hot oil. The guests would pop these crunchy pieces in their mouth all day long. Cajuns didn't seem to worry too much about their hearts, just their stomachs.

Raleigh grinned, though she was laughing inside her head. "Great guys. We may not have music yet, but we have the pigs and that's the most important thing."

"Yes'm," Ben nodded. "You know Kayla was supposed to be here today."

Flannel guy's head bobbed up and down. "I'm going to miss her. Sure was a sweet thing."

Raleigh tensed again. "Were you close?"

Ben shook his head. "Not really. We saw her often at Old Man Phil's bar. She was always nice then."

"When did you see her last?"

"Well, I reckon that'd be Monday," Ben looked toward the flannel guy and he nodded.

"She was a regular on Thursday nights, but we played our monthly Pedro game that night so we weren't there."

Raleigh nodded. So maybe Kayla had been there and had met her killer among the crowd.

Ben chuckled and pointed to the big tent. "I think your band just arrived."

Raleigh looked to see a pickup backing a trailer up to the make shift stage.

"Thanks, guys," Raleigh said, backing away. "Let me know if you need something." Raleigh headed back to the main tent.

"Why if it isn't Raleigh Cheramie," Jeffery Zedeaux said, emerging from an expensive-looking truck. The rotisserie had been on the edge of the party where the designated parking area started, and she could now see car after car pulling into the marked spots. The Ledets hadn't even stepped out of the main house towering over the empty field yet.

Raleigh cringed and did not plaster her usual smile. She didn't want him to get the impression that she actually liked him.

"I thought your sister would be working today. Actually, I thought you had some other low paying job besides this."

Raleigh gritted her teeth. He wouldn't be Jeffery without the cruel comment. "Madison called in sick. I'm just helping out."

He was wearing khaki slacks today and a blue pique cotton shirt. He must be trying to pass himself off as normal. His family money meant that he usually paraded around Barbeaux in a suit when everyone else wore jeans from Wal-Mart.

"Always helping aren't you." Jeffery shook his head. "I bet Mason would enjoy a party like this, but I guess he's used to being left behind."

Raleigh glared at him. She didn't have time to decipher his jerky commentary today. "I'm working Jeffery. I wish I could say it was a pleasure, but it never is."

Raleigh turned on her black-heeled boot and headed toward the band.

Several cars had begun to line up behind the tent in what Raleigh was sure would be a full yard in an hour. She'd approached the band's trailer when a brunette caught her attention.

Raleigh stopped and stared at the petite woman sauntering toward a hunter green Ford. In profile, it appeared to be Madison. The Madison who'd called in sick today and was the reason she was working on her morning off.

The brunette turned briefly toward her as she stepped up to the opened window. A man's hand, clutching a thick manila envelope, reached out. Madison's look alike clasped the envelope, scanning the parking area. Even with the heavy black sunglasses, Raleigh recognized Madison when she pursed her lips together.

Raleigh walked towards the truck, quickening her pace even as Madison turned and darted toward her car. Her driver door had been left open and waiting as if she wanted a quick getaway.

"Madison!" Raleigh called out. Madison didn't even look before the car lurched into drive and spun out toward the driveway. She was gone.

What had been in that envelope that was so important that she'd show up at a job she'd called in sick for? She could have come to work and at least be less conspicuous about it.

Raleigh had a feeling she didn't want to know what was in that envelope, but she was just as sure she was going to ask.

Six

Raleigh was as done as the grass on a Louisiana summer day. She wouldn't be screaming for the party to continue after all those hours on her feet, but the party still raged on behind her. Mrs. Ledet had kept the good times and beer flowing as the old people Cajun danced on the lawn, but thankfully, Raleigh had been able to call it quits after her job was done.

Her calf muscles trembled from exhaustion after hours of running around, but Mike still hadn't picked up his phone. He'd never gone this long without returning her calls, and it was driving her crazy. She considered running right out and buying a 'don't leave me even though I'm crazy present.' But what do you buy that would make that statement? She was at a loss for ideas. She'd feel better if he'd answer the phone and just tell her he was angry or upset or anything really. As long as he was talking to her, it didn't matter.

She headed toward the paper because Mike typically worked on Saturdays for a few hours in the afternoon preparing his weekend stories. She hoped he'd lost his phone like that one time in a cow incident he'd refused to explain. There'd been something about a cow pasture and his Jeep, but his face went blank and he refused to say anything more. Maybe he'd dropped it last night at the Dantin barn.

His white Jeep wasn't parked in the employee lot, but David's BMW occupied his usual space in front of the green "Editor" post. Maybe he'd know why Mike was playing hide-n-seek today or at least where he was.

David's office was a disaster; the kind left behind after floodwater's receded. Raleigh avoided the crumbling stacks of folders near the door and made her way around several boxes spilling their contents onto the floor.

"What happened here?" Raleigh stumbled over a box of old cassette tapes as David looked up from the red marked copy and marker he'd been taking serious frustration out on.

David's frown deepened and the line on his forehead sunk further inward. "I asked the college intern to go through some old files."

Raleigh raised her eyebrows in response, for he had to be talking about Aimee who'd quit yesterday afternoon because she wanted to go on some exotic Christmas vacation with her boyfriend. Maybe this mess had something to do with her willingness to give up college credit and her GPA. David shook his head and waved it off. It might be in her best interest to refrain from commenting or she'd be forced to clean the mess.

"Have you seen Mike today?"

"No," David set his pen down. "He usually comes in, but I haven't heard from him today. I've been waiting for the arrest records, damn Laurence not returning my calls. Supposed to have dinner with my wife."

"I think Mike is avoiding me," Raleigh said biting her lip. Where was he? He always came to work on Saturday. "He's not answering my calls."

"That doesn't sound like Mike," David leaned back in his chair, stretching his arms above his head. "How about you go down to the station and pick up the report for me instead of worrying about it. Larna has been giving me such a hard time lately about all the hours I work. If I'm late for dinner, I may have to uncover the couch in this office tonight."

Raleigh opened her mouth to protest, but he grinned. "Or you could clean the office for me instead while I go pick them up."

Raleigh chuckled. "That's low, but alright, I'll go. You will owe me though because I had enough of the station last night."

"Last night?" David pushed his glasses back up on his nose.

"A long story that involves another body. Mike and I will get you a story before deadline if he ever returns my calls."

David nodded. "I look forward to reading it." His chair creaked as he stood up. "I better get home before I really do have to clean off this sofa. She told me not to come home if I miss dinner tonight. You're a woman, what would you say that means?"

Raleigh laughed. Relationship advice – from her? He must be desperate. "It means you need to go home more often. Perhaps, stay home on a Saturday every now and then."

David smiled sheepishly as they exited the side door to the employee parking lot. "I could just hire her to clean my office, so she could see me all day at work."

Relationship expert, she wasn't, but she could imagine how well that would go over. One failed engagement and a boyfriend she wasn't sure was a boyfriend, did not give her the right to offer advice. It was reassuring that she wasn't the only one clueless about relationships though.

Ten minutes later, Raleigh pulled her car into the parking lot, leaving it idle as she stared at the lobby's big wall of windows. Barbeaux Police Station. Ugh. Could she hate a place more? She'd probably rank it above the muddy bayou she had an intense phobia of.

As she swung the car door open, a woozy feeling crashed in on her skull and darkness threatened. She clutched the door handle, inhaling long deep breaths. No! No more dead people in her head tonight. She deserved a break. She hadn't had time to forget the last one, so her head should be closed for business.

A sharp pain stabbed through her head, and her conscience (in Me'Maw's voice, of course) chided her. They connected to her because they needed her to listen.

Dammit. She couldn't get a break these days.

She closed her eyes and braced herself against the car. She didn't feel like wearing the parking lot's asphalt tonight.

The haziness didn't clear though. Shapes and colors blurred, attempting to sharpen, but couldn't. The images slipped into darkness like waking from a dream. Then the fuzziness began to clear, and she knew she wasn't going to connect.

But, then hazy smoke blurred her vision and her lungs seized as her nostrils filled with the sting. The smoke singed through her like burning paper before it evaporated and her head cleared, leaving her staring at the pavement.

Strange. No connection or dead body, just smoke. She'd learned over time that strange was never good.

She couldn't stand in the parking lot all day and try to figure it out though.

Inside the station, Raleigh noticed that every lolling officer stared at her as she walked in, but when she looked at them, their gaze dropped to the floor. Had they been watching her by the car and commented on her freakiness? It had to have grown old by now. Everyone knew about her weird ability to communicate with the dead.

Tyler stood behind the central desk, and his eyes darted everywhere but her as she approached. Tyler had lived at the front of Cheramie Lane as a baby. She'd babysat for him when he was in diapers, and she'd been eleven. She'd attempt not to have that image for the entire conversation. She'd try real hard.

His voice squeaked. "Can I help you, Ma'am?"

"Tyler, don't give me any of that." She bristled. Ma'am?

She wasn't old enough to be Ma'am. That was her mother and her grandmother, not her.

Tyler's face drooped and paled. Gosh, it wasn't that serious. She had a name, and it wasn't Ma'am, which hinted at kids, a house, and age. He knew her. That's all she meant by it.

"I've come to pick up the arrest records for the Sunday paper. They weren't sent on time today."

His shoulders sank and relief arrived with a grin. "Oh, thank goodness. I thought you were here about Mike."

Raleigh tapped on the counter. "Why would I be here about Mike?"

Tyler shrugged. "I thought he was your friend, and with him still being here, I thought you'd come to start some trouble like you usually do."

With each word, she thought just how wrong he was. She didn't even know where to start as anger surged though her.

"Was Mike arrested?"

His face paled again. "Not... not that I know of."

She could see the realization behind his shifty green eyes that he had just told her something she didn't know. He hadn't been so slow on the uptake when she'd had to chase his chubby legs racing around the house.

"So why is he still here?"

His gaze dropped to a sheet of notes on the desk. "I'm not really at liberty to give out that information."

Raleigh slapped her hand down on the counter and he jumped. "Tyler, I changed your diapers and chased you around your mother's living room. Don't you tell me you're not at liberty. Where's Max?"

Raleigh scanned the station. Everyone in the station was openly gaping at them. She had the feeling in the pit of her stomach that she would regret this later.

"I'm afraid he's busy right now."

But regret wasn't among the many emotions surging through her right this minute. The blinds in Max's office were semi-closed, but she could see him leaning over his desk.

"Max!" Tyler rose with a lurch from his chair. "Maxwell Pyles, you come out here!"

Several doors popped open and more onlookers emerged from behind the doors. Raleigh watched as Max stood and crossed to his closed door.

The office door next to Max's swung open first, and William Blanch popped his head out. "What's going on out here?"

"I'm sorry, sir." Tyler gulped and stumbled over his words.

Finally, Max's door swung open.

"Max, why is Mike still being held?"

Raleigh's body trembled. In a small part of her brain, she registered the combination of circumstances fueling her anger. There was the simple humiliation of a scene, the anger that Mike had been detained and no one knew, and the fact that Max had kept it from her. She wasn't sure which one angered her more at this point.

Max's normal hypnotic gaze wasn't working on her through her anger. The intenseness of his glare should scare her, but the part that cared was buried somewhere deep.

"My office," he said, swinging the door wide open for her.

Raleigh crossed toward the door. The only sound in the walk that felt like it took two months was someone coughing, which only added to the embarrassment of everyone watching her.

He closed the door behind her, and she waited for the click.

"Why the hell is Mike still here, and when did you plan to tell me?"

"Mike is the primary suspect in a murder investigation. Police business isn't open for discussion."

His formal tone stung more than she'd like. "Mike is not a murderer, and you know it."

"No," he said, sitting behind his desk. "No, I don't know. What I do know is that the victim had a relationship with Mike. A relationship that witnesses say ended ugly. I'm going on facts and evidence here."

"There was no relationship," Raleigh said. Frustration was now overwhelming her anger. Why was he talking about facts and evidence on someone he knew? "Mike has a three date rule; one girl no more than three times. Kayla wasn't any different."

"I have witnesses at work, a restaurant and a bar that say it was a relationship that ended badly just this week."

"It wasn't a relationship! Why aren't you listening to me?" Raleigh's frustration was burning her up. "She stalked Mike. She showed up at his house in the middle of the night. He told her to leave him alone."

"All the more reason that he is a possible suspect."

"Then so am I," Raleigh said, sinking into the chair in the front of the desk. "So take me in for questioning as well."

"Don't be ridiculous."

"I was with Mike at the time she was killed, when she was buried, and when we found her. If he is a suspect, then I am his accomplice."

"Watch who you say that to," he said meeting her glare. She didn't look away, so they stared at each other, unflinching. Her face burned, but she would not back down on this.

He dropped the gaze first. "Look, I realize that Mike probably didn't do it, but it does look very bad for him. Did you see anything that would help?"

Raleigh shook her head. She hadn't missed the

"probably". Doubt. "It was weird. She was dead nearly twenty-four hours before I connected to her, and that's just not how it's done."

Max nodded, but his attention was far away. His gray eyes were unfocused as they'd often been in the last month. She'd learned to pick up on these little things, but she couldn't say much past his son, his thoughts on his family, and his love of his career. She still didn't know him well.

He reached over, picked up the phone, and spoke tersely into the phone about releasing Mike.

After he hung up, Raleigh smiled. A peace offering. "Thank you."

"It's not going to go away that easy," Max warned.

Raleigh stood. "Nothing ever does."

She opened the door watching for Mike to exit through the back security door.

Detective Blanch barreled out of his office toward her. His glare only scorched through her a moment. "Max, you have no right to interfere with my case."

"You can't hold a witness unless you charge him with something. Mike is free to go. I simply reminded Max, and now you, of that simple legal fact."

Raleigh caught the momentary gratefulness flash in Max's eyes before he turned to Detective Blanch and shrugged his shoulders. "Ms. Cheramie has knowledge of the system, Will."

Mike emerged from the back steal door. His angular face held dark circles and drooped. His naturally easy smile had disappeared into an out-of-place grimace.

With everyone watching them, Raleigh fought the urge to sweep him into a hug. But he looked like he needed it. The tension in the station rose from the floors and rooted everyone to their spots as they were forced to watch Raleigh rescue Mike with Max, her new beau, watching.

Interesting circumstances.

"Excuse me," the tension broke with the intrusion of a pretty blond who'd approached unnoticed. "Max, I'd like a moment if you aren't busy."

Max nodded his head and moved to the side so she could walk into his office. She smiled and breezed through everyone. Who was she and why was she calling him by his first name? She was fair complected, slightly taller than Raleigh was, and beautiful in that put together way that Raleigh would never achieve even if a personal hair stylist and make-up artist trailed her.

"I suggest you stay in Barbeaux," Blanch grumbled through his teeth. "I will be bringing you back in as soon as I can."

Raleigh grabbed Mike's arm and steered him out of the fray. He stumbled along behind her, half-awake. She looked back as Max closed his office door behind them. She better be someone from a case, preferably a suspect, but then again, that's how they'd met.

Seven

The one street lamp Mike's dead end street offered left much to the imagination with the shadows the dull glow created. Raleigh eased her car into the driveway and sat looking at Mike's shotgun house. The green box house could have fit in a normal size living room, but the narrow yard was trimmed and clean. Similar houses rubbed shoulders with each other up and down the street. Most of the houses were rent houses or still belonged to the people who'd built them sixty years ago. She looked over at Mike who was slumped in the passenger seat with eyelids drooped. He'd stopped trying to keep them open two streets down.

Raleigh patted his leg. "Go get some sleep. I'll bring you to get your Jeep after my date tonight."

"You deserve better," Mike grumbled. "If a guy skips out on half your dates, he's not good enough for you."

Raleigh rubbed the indention of the scar on her wrist. Good natured Mike hid somewhere inside the cranky sleep deprived version. But he had a point. Making half the dates would be better statistics. Out of nine dates, Max had managed to keep four. If he remembered their date tonight, they'd hit a percentage of half, but if he canceled again, the statistics would hit an all-time low.

"Max is just busy with work." But the awful statistics didn't stop Raleigh from wanting things to turn out differently each time. Sad fact, but true.

"If that makes you feel better," Mike grumbled, swinging the door open. "I'll call you later."

She wasn't going to take it personally. Grumpy Mike didn't show his face often, and she still couldn't believe they'd kept him twenty-four hours. He deserved to be cranky and unhappy with Max. In fact, dinner conversation might be a bit strained since she had her own anger over the whole ordeal she hadn't dealt with yet.

On the way up the one lane road, she had to pull over into T-Boy's yard to allow a police cruiser to pass. Police cruisers didn't come down these streets unless they were called to a house. In the rearview mirror, she watched the car pullover and park. Dammit. They'd put Mike under surveillance. Any chance of her anger dissipating had disappeared into thin air.

Raleigh gritted her teeth and drove to the newspaper instead of beating the police car with her tire iron. After she maneuvered around the clutter, she placed the arrest records on David's desk. He'd come in later and place them on the page because he had this craziness about the Sunday paper going to print early. Larna would not like their dinner plans ending with more office time, and he may have to spend the night here after all.

Oh, what the heck. She could be generous since she was already here. Entering the information into David's computer, she stopped as she recognized Winter's name third on the list. Disorderly conduct didn't really sound like Winter. Summer, maybe. Summer had a reputation for causing a scene or inciting a fight between men battling for her attention. Winter could be trying to keep her friend alive.

"Arrest records, I see," David said. She jumped and the chair creaked beneath her.

"I thought I'd get it done so you could end the night with your wife."

"Good, good." David nodded. "I forgot the tickets to the art show. Good I don't have to come back again tonight. Send it when you're done, please."

Raleigh studied him a moment. Something must be wrong. "Is everything alright?"

"Splendid," he nodded and frowned, his head in a deep bow. "She made me agree to counseling. Not sure how it could get worse, so it's good."

Raleigh hid her laugh with a cough. This was what she was missing by being an old maid at twenty-nine by bayou standards. Social misfit looked better and better.

"I know," his head dipped further until she could only see his mop of chestnut hair. "I'm in trouble."

Raleigh pressed submit and walked out with David. "Everything will be fine, David. Just show up for a few dates."

That was about the extent of her advice. She couldn't be the only woman who wanted a date to actually, you know, show up.

Seven minutes later she reached Cheramie Lane and dialed Madison's number to no avail. After eleven calls today, Raleigh should just assume the girl wasn't going to answer. What the girl did with herself all day was the prize-winning question. Topping the list was what had she done to get herself into trouble. It was never a good sign when Madison avoided her.

Raleigh entered the back door into Me'Maw's kitchen by passing the family Labrador, Spencer, who didn't so much as move an ear. Was it possible he'd gone deaf as well as arthritic? Inside the kitchen, the aroma of Cajun food didn't engulf her, so she looked toward the stove and didn't see a bubbling pot on the stove. She noticed the grim expressions on her grandparent's faces and all sorts of warning bells clanged in her head.

"We'll scrounge up the money somewhere 'dis month." Paw said as she eased the snap of the screen door behind her.

Me'Maw's rocking chair was still. Usually it creaked as it went up and down in her normal rhythm. "I could ask for donations from my regulars."

Raleigh's mouth opened and her heart slammed into her chest though she still stood in the doorway. Had she walked into a different universe? Me'Maw had never taken payment for her traiteur sessions since she'd started at seventeen years old. People dropped off fresh chicken eggs or a basket of oranges, but never money. Traiteurs didn't take money as tradition, and Me'Maw followed the old ways down to the handwritten recipes passed on to her.

Paw shook his head, though he rubbed the stubble on his chin at the same time. "You can't do that, Ma. Joey wants me to work on his tractor. I'll ask him for money this time."

Me'Maw's chest hunched over until it was nearly in her lap. "I hate having to ask him. You know he doesn't make much at the sheriff's office."

Raleigh's heart felt as if it were really being wrung like an old dishtowel. Had she missed that they were having hard times while she was living in their house?

"Paw, if you need money, I can pitch in more. I get paid Tuesday, so just tell me what you need."

"Nonsense," Me'Maw said, but her head didn't lift from its position. "You already give me money every month for groceries and what not. That's not where we're coming up short."

"Where then?" Raleigh asked, but then bit down on her lip, a sharp pain shooting through her. Paw would say she was meddling in his business. Paw didn't like meddling of any kind.

She looked at him, but he didn't look at her or move or speak. Now she'd done it.

Me'Maw sighed a deep release from her chest that rattled. "We've been taking care of Aunt Clarice's old house payment the last three months. Our fixed income isn't stretching that far, I'm afraid."

"Why isn't Madison paying it?"

Me'Maw answered with silence. She kept sticking her

foot further in her mouth.

Paw stood up from his seat at the table; his navy Dickies slightly dusty with a layer of dirt that had probably blown up from his garden. "It's time for my evening walk in the garden."

Raleigh remained quiet until the screen door slammed behind him. At least he hadn't told her to take a walk with him through the rows. That's when she knew it was bad.

"I'm sorry, Me'Maw," Raleigh said. "Can't Madison afford the note anymore?"

Me'Maw rocked forward and it creaked against the wooden floor. "Just a little trouble between the car note and Mason's daycare expenses. She got behind with taking that time off from work and all. It'll be fine soon, I'm sure."

Raleigh thought it better to drop it, so she walked toward her bedroom before temptation won out. She'd learned last month that the mortgage payment was $350. When someone had wanted to rent it out, Paw had said no because he wasn't a Cheramie. Cheramie houses should have Cheramies in it, and it wasn't negotiable with him. That was a stiff payment for two people living on a fixed income though. Madison had to know this. She'd add it to that growing list of questions for her sister if she ever picked up her phone.

Back in her bedroom, she dialed Madison's number as she scanned the mess in her room. Boxes crowded the room as usual, but stacks of clothes had toppled over again. The phone rang unanswered and now Raleigh hovered between angry and worried. Madison had been dancing on the bar just last night, so maybe she was back to her old ways; the old ways that left her skirting on the edge of prison or death.

Madison had sworn she'd changed though. She'd sat on Raleigh's bed last month and swore she wanted to do things the right way.

Raleigh was doing it again - spending too much time worrying about her sister. Didn't she have her own life?

Yes, and she had an hour before her date. The whole town would soon gossip about whatever Madison was doing. She was sure to find out then. For now she needed to shower.

An hour and a half later, Raleigh tossed piles of clothes into an empty box, seething. Max hadn't shown up or called. At least every time before when he'd missed the date, he'd called and said something had come up at work. No call. Nothing. Raleigh stuffed more clothes in the box, wondering why she'd bothered making a date with him.

The coarse shrill of her cell rumbled from her white bed coverings.

Relief flooded through her, relaxing her shoulders. He must be running late and was calling to let her know. He'd promised he'd show up this time no matter what came up. It had to be him.

As she fetched it from the bed, her heart sank as Mike Simmon's name filled the screen. Mike never forgot to call even when he wasn't the one she wanted to hear from.

"Ree, Jeff said he'd bring me if you were busy."

Raleigh huffed as she realized she'd never be able to find anything that she'd stuck into every nook and cranny her messy room offered. She shouldn't be organizing when angry.

"I'll go. Max didn't show, so I'm sure he's not coming."

He answered with silence. He'd held his comments, which meant he'd slept the last few hours away. Good. Laid back Mike was more fun when a person had been stood up.

"I'll see you in a few minutes," Raleigh said, before hanging up. She'd save him from saying 'I told you so.' She already knew it anyway.

On her way out, she bent down to pick up a ripped piece of paper that had fallen from an old dresser. Madison's bubble letters filled the page. "If anyone asks, I was with you two nights ago. Madison."

That feeling you get when you're five and you've broken your mother's glass vase, and you know you are in big trouble shot through her now. Even though it was Madison's trouble, she knew some how she'd be included in the punishment. Wasn't that how it went?

Eight

"Tell him no; tell him you're busy," Mike said as she parked her car next to his Jeep. "Just make him wait... a long time."

She'd of course told Mike about the date and the dismal statistics. She'd always told him everything, and to his credit, he had remained silent, mostly. He'd made his point though: she was making it too easy for Max. It just wasn't what she wanted to hear tonight when her pride was hurt yet again.

"I'm not interested in games."

Mike stared at her. She could feel his eyes on her, and she knew he was waiting for her to look at him. She relented. "Don't let him walk all over you. You deserve to be his priority."

Tears stung the back of her eyes and burned her throat. Dammit. She looked away from him. When had he become so sensitive? As an only child, he didn't even have sisters. Of course, his two best friends in school had been female so something must have rubbed off during that time.

She looked toward the station to do something with herself. The lights from the glass windows spilled out into the darkness, creating shadows in the poorly lit parking lot.

"Three nights at this place really isn't good for our reputations."

Mike chuckled. "Our reputations were shot to hell a long time ago. People think it's normal for us."

Raleigh laughed, despite the sadness weighing on her, and the tension in the car eased. Behind the glass two figures stood with their heads bent toward each other in deep conversation. Their shadows loomed over the light filtering into the parking lot.

Mike swung the car door open, and the figures both

turned to identify the movement outside. Max and the pretty blonde from earlier now stared at her. She was the reason he hadn't shown up. The thought burned through her.

She got out the car and crossed the hundred feet to the door. She wasn't sure what she was doing, but she couldn't help herself.

The door buzzed as she swung it open. She could feel his eyes on her, but Raleigh couldn't stop looking at the woman. She had those innocent blue eyes, porcelain skin, and the blonde hair that was probably, called Blonde Ambition or something vulgar like that. She'd probably been told her entire life she was beautiful, but she still needed to hear it. Her big wide eyes and tilted heart shaped face annoyed Raleigh on sight.

She turned away from the siren and met Max's gaze. He adjusted his stance a few inches, sweeping a quick look at the white-faced clock.

"Too busy to call this time?" Raleigh said, the words slipping out beneath her clinched jaw. She didn't like the anger in them and the feeling they left behind.

The woman looked to him, her eyes sympathetic and pleading at once for him to look at her, don't be mad at her, or whatever sexual desire she'd imagined for the two of them. Raleigh felt nauseated. Damn, she hated her.

She pushed back through the door and allowed it to swing shut behind her with a loud clash.

Mike waited ten feet from the door, absorbing it all. His jaw was clenched, but his spine was slouched in his normal laid back way with his hands hanging from his pockets. "Jeff and Sheri are at Roxy's shooting pool. I say we could both use a little fun tonight."

Raleigh nodded, wondering if fun was even an option tonight. She couldn't even decide if she was upset or angry. The line was as blurry as chocolate milk, make that a mudslide. Her emotions were a nice even mixture of everything swirling around.

They'd only made it a few steps when the station door swung open.

"How can you be so arrogant!" the young blonde huffed. "What kind of monster just flaunts himself in public after murdering someone?"

A slight pitch of hysteria tinged her voice, and the hint of craziness sent a chill up Raleigh's spine.

Mike's fist clenched. "I haven't murdered anyone."

"Liar," the woman screeched. "You killed her. She loved you and you killed her."

The door swung open again and Max stepped outside. The young woman threw herself against Max's chest, her fingers clutching at his chest as she sobbed hysterically.

Raleigh tensed and her insides trembled. Max didn't push her away. He didn't wrap his arm around her, but he did pat her shoulder. The smell of the woman's perfume reached Raleigh's senses and stung her eyes, her nose, and her throat. Her eyes watered and Max and the blonde blurred into black spots before her. She felt the scene before her tilt. Drunk. She felt as if she was intoxicated beyond any normal limit she'd ever experienced.

Mike reached out and gripped her elbow. "Are you alright?"

Raleigh stepped back, feeling Mike's grip stiffen on her elbow, as tears blurred her vision even more. She refused to connect to the dead here, not with everyone watching. A brisk wind swept up her hair and whipped it around. It gusted again, sweeping the strong perfume smell away. The burning in her eyes eased.

Good. She could feel it clearing. It must be the perfume triggering a connection. Everything about this death was strange. It left her hoping that the connections would go back to normal, and that she'd thought she'd never say.

"Let's get out of here," Raleigh said, turning away from Max. He hadn't removed her from his personal space, and she was standing right in front of him.

She waved Mike's concern away and lowered her trembling self into her car. She took a deep breath, easing some of the shaking in her legs before starting the car and following Mike's Jeep to Roxy's. She forced herself not to look back at Max. How was that for self-control? Even her best friend Cassie had given up on her ever possessing it. She'd be real proud if she'd seen this but she lived all the way in Baton Rouge.

Six cars were parked out front in the shell parking lot of Roxy's. She checked her face and hair in the rearview mirror. Her already pale skin appeared paler, her amber eyes too wide, and those three freckles too bright but otherwise it wasn't too bad. At least her hair cooperated these days with Sheri's expert help.

Mike opened her car door for her. "What was that?"

"Her perfume triggered some kind of weird connection. I don't know what that means."

Mike nodded. "At least no new bodies tonight."

"I'll drink to that," Raleigh said, as Mike opened the door.

Inside, Sheri and Jeff sipped beer from large glass mugs at the bar. Roxy's insides were sparse and bordering on decrepit. Once white paneling graced the walls and appeared dirtier under the muted brown stained light bulbs. To her left were the empty pool tables and only one of the four booths against the right wall had people. The place had nine patrons and a bartender. The opening weekend of *The Seafood Camp* had put a damper on the place that was normally filled wall to wall with regulars.

Jeff made a motion for the bartender to bring drinks to

them as they slid onto bar stools. Within minutes, mugs were placed before them.

Raleigh sipped tentatively in hopes of easing the tension she felt through her spine, but her insides quivered as it slid down. Not a hint of chocolate in that glass. It just wasn't her night.

Jeff rested his empty mug on top of the scuffed bar top. "How about a game of pool to liven this place up a bit?"

"No," Raleigh protested. "I'm horrible."

Sheri chuckled. "Yes, we'd need to wear body armor to stand near."

Raleigh blushed. "That only happened once."

Mike laughed, squeezing her shoulder. "No, it didn't."

Raleigh laughed, using the moment to scan the bar. The same patrons sat in the booth, but as she returned her attention to the bar, she spotted Madison at the opposite end of the bar folding napkins. How had she not noticed her?

Raleigh stood, her eyes on Madison's dark hair bent over the table. "Give me a moment, guys."

Mike tugged her jean's pocket. "Go easy..."

Raleigh looked down at Mike and caught the twitching of his lip. "She..."

"... on yourself." The twitch went full grin.

Raleigh squeezed his hand before walking toward Madison. Raleigh made it half way there before Madison looked up from her napkin folding. A soft flicker shone briefly in her eyes, but she quickly emptied her face of any emotion. It wasn't an excited to see her big sister kind of look.

"I've tried to reach you all day," Raleigh said.

Madison didn't respond. Her hands fumbled with the napkin in her hands. Raleigh waited in the growing silence. "I can't find my phone."

Madison usually had that purple phone glued to her hands. Raleigh exhaled, reminding herself that there were bigger issues to argue over, and she was certain this was going to be one of them.

"What's going on with you?"

Madison didn't skip a beat with the folding. "What do you mean?"

"You called in sick for the boucherie, yet I see you in the parking lot. Then I get a note as if you need an alibi two nights ago. What's going on?"

"I wasn't at the boucherie," Madison said, fumbling with the napkin. Her hands quivered, and Raleigh could tell she was trying hard to steady herself.

"Madison, I think I would recognize my own sister. I saw you when *I* had to take *your* place."

Madison abandoned the napkin folding and pierced Raleigh with those eyes that were only a slight shade lighter than her own were, but always more intense. "I picked something up in the parking lot. Are you spying on me?"

"It's not spying," Raleigh said. Every encounter with Madison made her feel twelve years old again. The six-year-old Madison hadn't been any easier to get through to. "What is going on with you? You are never home, but you aren't at work. You ask me to cover for you. Me'Maw and Paw are paying your bills. How can you do that to them?"

"My life is none of your business," Madison's eyes flashed. Madison's lip always curled to the right when she was angry, and it was in full curl at the moment. Raleigh knew she should back off, but dammit this was too important.

"Your son is always at Me'Maw's, I'm always covering for you at work, and you are asking me to lie and say you were home. It definitely is my business."

"Then don't," Madison spit out. "Don't do any of it. You

take my place at work for the money, not for me. So don't play the poor pitiful Raleigh card. Me'Maw watches Mason, so if you don't want him around, move out. Forget about me asking for an alibi, I should have known better than to ask goody two shoes for a favor."

"Are you in trouble?"

Madison stepped back. Raleigh would have sworn that fear had flashed through her eyes. "Don't worry about it; I can take care of myself. I don't need you to save me."

"What's wrong with you?"

"Life." Madison's shoulders sank. "It's hard."

"Madison, you can ask for help."

"Raleigh, just leave it alone." Madison grabbed another napkin and began folding.

"Me'Maw and Paw can't afford to pay the house note. They don't have the money."

"Then the bank can take it."

Raleigh's stomach clenched. "It would kill Paw to let another Cheramie house go."

"Whatever, Raleigh," Madison snapped. "You're such the favorite, why don't you figure out how to pay for it."

Frustration welled inside. It was like talking to the wall, but the wall wasn't quite so irritating.

Raleigh's cell phone vibrated in her pocket. She hesitated picking it up. She'd gotten nowhere with Madison. She glanced down and saw Cassie's name on the screen. Cassie wasn't typically home making phone calls on a Saturday night.

"It's not my birthday, so what's up?"

Silence greeted her. Not a good sign.

Cassie's voice came through after a few uncertain heartbeats, but it held that sharp edge it took on when she was speaking to unrealistic clients. "We need to talk. Are you alone?"

Raleigh's body began to warm, preparing for bad news. "I will be in a moment." Raleigh glanced at Madison, who buried her face behind her hair as she folded. Madison wouldn't be saying anything else tonight. It was her way.

Raleigh stepped out the front door of Roxy's and into the crisp night air. The chilly air caused her to shiver, but the night offered silence as well.

"What's going on?"

Cassie's deep breath came through the phone. "A couple of weeks ago I ran into Glenn. He was looking for you."

Raleigh couldn't breath. Her lungs refused to inhale or exhale. "A couple of weeks ago?"

"Let me finish," Cassie said, her tone chastising. Cassie didn't like to be questioned- or interrupted. "I told him that you didn't want to see him and that he needed to stop trying."

Raleigh inhaled, easing the pain spreading through her chest. She croaked out, "Thank you."

"I'm not finished." Raleigh's chest tightened and then tingled. Dread filled her from her toes.

"I ran into Mr. Grabert today, you know your old boss. Glenn found him as well, but he didn't know anything, so he told him you had gone back home."

"No." Raleigh inhaled sharply. Weeks. Weeks had gone by where Glenn knew where she lived. Barbeaux Bayou was only a two hour drive from Baton Rouge, not so far if you've already driven from Houston. He'd traveled all that distance. Why hadn't he given up?

"Raleigh, you need to face him. Just tell him face to face that you don't want anything to do with him anymore."

"I don't want to." Raleigh detected the slight whine in her own voice. The shame didn't overpower her lack of courage on this one. "If I would have wanted to do that I wouldn't have left in the middle of the night."

"You sound like a child, Raleigh Lynn." Cassie's tone was sharp, but then she sighed. "Okay, don't do it alone then. Ask Mike to help. But if you want him to leave you alone, you are going to have to be the one to tell him."

"I know," Raleigh said, her heart raced at the consent. The humiliation still rested close to the surface. She'd be married to him now, but there'd been the dead body. The humiliation had only begun there though; the snowball effect began with the dead girl. Why did all her trouble begin with dead bodies?

"Maybe he's given up. How many people actually travel to Barbeaux Bayou?"

"You did," Cassie said. "You don't seem to be leaving anytime soon either."

True, but she came from here. Her family was here. Glenn's mother lived in Austin. "Where am I going to go? I don't know any place else."

"Mess seems to follow you; you know that's not normal, right?" She sighed and continued in a softer tone. "You know I love you anyway, right?"

Raleigh rolled her eyes, realizing she wasn't twelve and that Cassie couldn't see her. Any affection from strong-willed Cassie made her uncomfortable. Thankfully, it didn't come often, but there was never a question it was there. Who else would try to create self-improvement plans for her? Type A personality herself.

"Yes, yes, I know." Raleigh agreed. "I'll keep you up to date."

"You better," Cassie added. "It's the only drama I get these days with my hours at work."

Raleigh hung up and nausea overwhelmed her. The smell of dirty water filled her throat, her nose, and her mouth. She was going to be sick.

Her stomach churned. She felt the intoxication of one more glass than she should have. The gravel began to spin; she closed her eyes to it. The bloodshot eyes of Kayla met her behind her eyelids.

Her heart leapt forward in her chest and her eyes sprang open. Beside from her racing heart, her body returned to normal.

She'd connected to Kayla? How? It didn't work that way. Dammit, if she had to live with this connection, the rules had to quit changing.

She couldn't push those bloodshot eyes away. She hadn't looked close enough last night to see if it was real or she'd imagined them. She couldn't have imagined it though. It had been so familiar moments ago.

Right?

Her scalp prickled. Recognition seeped into each cell of her body, clinching her muscles tight.

She'd seen those bloodshot eyes on another body. The woman's body in Houston the night she'd discovered who Glenn really was.

Chills ran through her. It had to be a coincidence. Two bodies found in shallow graves had to happen more than once in the history of crazy psycho killers. Right? She didn't believe in coincidences though.

Nine

Raleigh slowed as she came to Aunt Clarice's old house on Cheramie Lane. She'd loved that house with its gallery porch and stained glass dormer window above since she was a little girl. In Me'Maw's house they'd run through the scuffed floors, but not here. Small trinkets from around the world filled shelves and glass cabinets, and Raleigh had studied some odd or end each time, careful not to mark or leave footprints on the floor between the oriental rugs. Each trinket had a mesmerizing story to add to the eccentricity of the glass skull or porcelain teacup or ivory carved elephant or whatever new discovery she'd made.

None of those things had been out the last time she'd been in the house. She wondered if Madison had tossed it all or saved any of it. Madison had always thought of it all as clutter. It made her sad that she hadn't been here to salvage any of Aunt Clarice's items.

She eased her car next to Max's Caprice parked crooked in Me'Maw's driveway. How long had he waited for her? A twang of guilt throbbed in her chest, but it eased after she thought about their missing date. Not even a phone call or a text this time. And what about the woman? Did he get involved with all single women on his cases? That question nagged at her and wouldn't go away.

"I waited for you," he said. "I hope you don't mind." His eyes were like warm honey, reeling her in. She'd swear he had hypnotizing skills.

She felt her resolve washing away in his gaze. Dammit. Her eyes fell to the sexy way his polo shirt tugged at his arms and shoulders and how his normally relaxed stance was tense.

Her face heated. This wasn't helping her resolve.

"I didn't expect you to show up," Raleigh said, her voice

a whisper. She didn't trust herself to speak. Her thin grasp on her anger was loosening, and she didn't want to forgive him yet or maybe at all. Her head and heart argued about it with no clear winner.

"I'm here to apologize. I know I'm always using work as an excuse, but the case has monopolized everything- my time, my thoughts, everything." He quieted, and his gaze focused somewhere behind her. "But it's difficult when you become involved in my cases."

She felt a distance between them with those eyes not warming her. "How does my telling you where the body is make it difficult?"

The tension in the three-foot space between them was thick enough to touch. "It's not that. Not everyone accepts your stories as I do. My credibility suffers."

"Stories?" Her face heated, and the anger traveled downward through her body, dampening any sexual tension his eyes typically sparked.

"Don't do that, Raleigh." His eyes met hers again; they appeared to be pleading with her. Not a request she usually received. "Everyone believes Mike is responsible, and they are determined to prove it. I can't take the lead because of you, and that doesn't look good for Mike."

"Mike didn't murder her. I was with him." Even as she said it, she knew that would not help. They'd also been together when Raleigh had pulled the trigger in high school. The two of them weren't well liked by the Barbeaux police.

"I know." Max's eyes were deep pools of gray. "But it won't matter if Will Blanch won't listen. The order is that I'm off any cases you are connected to from now on, so they won't listen to me either."

"Mike didn't do this. I wouldn't lie for him." Raleigh's stomach squirmed. Would she lie for him? She might. She wasn't right now, but she was closer to him than anyone.

Max remained quiet moments longer than belief allowed. Did he think that as well?

"I don't believe Mike's capable of murder, but that's not the question here. They will focus on Mike until other suspects turn up, but they aren't looking for others."

"So if I give them another suspect, they would leave Mike alone?"

"Maybe. They'd have to rule Mike out first. Do you have another suspect?"

"Glenn Miller."

"Who's that?"

Raleigh's stomach flipped inside out. She hadn't thought this through. They'd never had this discussion or many others due to their lack of actual dates. How could she explain this now? "He was my fiancé until I discovered the body of his dead secretary/lover on a construction site buried similar to Kayla."

Max's expression didn't change. No movement of the eyes or a crinkling on his forehead or movement near his lips. "Did he kill her?"

Raleigh shrugged. "The police let him go. Later, I heard they didn't have enough evidence to charge him with the murder. I left after he was arrested, so I'm not sure what happened."

Max ran his hand through his cropped hair. He normally gelled it into place, but by this time of the day, it was loose and finger-combed. "Don't you think you should have mentioned this before? What other secrets do you have buried in the past?"

Raleigh stepped back from him. His anger had reached through his words and scorched her. "When was I supposed to mention it? On the date you forgot about or at the crime scene when you ignored me?"

He looked at her, his eyes giving away nothing. Raleigh

seethed. Maybe things between them were just too difficult.

"I'm sorry, but," he said, looking away, "I just don't like to be blindsided, and your past keeps colliding with my cases."

Raleigh squared her shoulders and tried to push away the current that ran between them even when they were arguing. She could be strong, for once in her life at least. "Apologies followed with a but don't really mean anything. Good night, Max."

She slipped in the front door and closed it behind her. His words nagged at her. She hadn't asked for Glenn to cheat on her with his secretary during their entire relationship. She certainly hadn't wanted to be the one who discovered the body with Glenn's cell phone laying two feet from it. The police had spelled out every last stomach turning detail to her, and she'd had to remind herself to breathe for a week. She'd escaped to Baton Rouge to cower in her humiliation and to hide. She hadn't wanted to think about Glenn, much less tell Max about him when he couldn't remember they were dating.

A loud screech shattered her deep thoughts and she was forced to rise from her lean to pose against the front door. Mason ran through the living room giggling.

"Mason Cheramie I told you five times to go to bed," Me'Maw's voice called from the kitchen.

Raleigh groaned. Why was Mason here? Had Madison forgotten about coming home now? She loved her nephew but quiet ranked about even with the massive ball of energy and noise that he created.

"I don't want to," Mason said, throwing himself on the sofa. Pillows flew onto the floor and the leather slapped against his pajamas.

"Mason," Raleigh's voice sounded sharper than she'd intended to so she swallowed and steadied herself before continuing. "Get to bed pronto. When Me'Maw speaks to you, your job is to listen."

Mason looked up at her from his face down position on the sofa. His big blue eyes widened and then his bottom lip began to tremble. He jumped up and ran down the hall to the spare bedroom that he slept in when he was here.

Raleigh closed her eyes. Longest day ever-- in her life. Maybe she needed to go to her own bed.

She ventured into the kitchen to find Me'Maw slumped in her favorite corner rocking chair. Her eyelids drooped and her velvety skin crinkled like the delicate pattern of a fingerprint. Me'Maw's worn deck of cards, the blue ink fading, rested at the small side table. Raleigh's eyes soaked in the whitened corner where Me'Maw's fingers had worn the blue away. If they were near her, Me'Maw had used them. Dread struck her in her chest. Any curiosity of what the cards held was tempered by an ominous feeling emitting from Me'Maw's countenance.

"Where's Mom and Dad?"

Me'Maw rocked forward and stopped. Her clear blue eyes looked up. "They went to that casino in Mississippi for the night."

"Where's Madison?" Raleigh asked, easing into the chair at the table. She'd left Madison at the bar, but what she really wanted to know was where had Madison told everyone she'd be.

"Work or something, I'm sure," Me'Maw said, looking down at the wooden floor beneath her rocker.

Raleigh sighed. Even as an adult, she felt guilty for snitching on someone. How was that? "Me'Maw, Madison is rarely where she says she is. Someone needs to talk to her about the choices she's making, but she doesn't want to hear it from me."

Me'Maw's rocker creaked as she leaned back. "She's just having a difficult time after everything that went on. She needs time to adjust and then she'll be okay."

"She needs someone to tell her she's acting like a teenager." And Raleigh should know. She felt like a teenager on a regular basis.

Me'Maw's rocking picked up speed. "She'll be alright. She just needs time to get everything together, and you two are nothing alike. You are much stronger and more independent."

Figures, Me'Maw had followed her thoughts. Madison always had the family helping her, making excuses. It was part of the problem. She'd never learn independence unless she was forced to. Apparently, it wasn't going to happen tonight. "Well, I'm going to bed. Paw sleeping already?"

"No, he's helping Joey tonight."

Raleigh turned back to look at Me'Maw. "It's late to be working on a tractor."

Me'Maw continued rocking though the pace slowed. "It's in the barn, so the dark doesn't matter."

What Raleigh had meant was that it was too late for Paw to be out in the chill of the December night air, and this was way past his 8:00 bedtime. None of that would have mattered either. Paw needed the money, and he would make sure the house wasn't lost to the bank even if it killed him in the process.

Something needed to be done about this situation before that's exactly what happened.

She walked down the darkened hall and stopped in the spare bedroom's doorway. Mason had the old quilt pushed up all the way under his chin. His eyes squinting closed, and from his erratic breathing she could tell he was pretending to sleep.

"Good night, Mason," Raleigh said, listening to his silence.

"Nite, Nanan," He finally said. He turned and buried his

head in a quilt.

"Love you."

"Love you too, Nanan," he said. "Tell Mommy I didn't get to stay up late like she promised me."

Madison. What would she do with Madison? Folding napkins couldn't pay that well, and she hadn't worried about Me'Maw babysitting this late either.

"I'll tell her."

He burrowed deeper into the blankets and his breathing shifted. Sleep for real.

What was Madison up to? It had to be something not good. Secretive people usually weren't up to good somethings. And everything kept adding up to Madison being guilty of something.

Max's admission that she would need to have other suspects to draw the suspicion away from Mike, left a strong uneasiness in her stomach. She had all the ingredients of a soap opera on her hands these days.

Ten

Raleigh sunk deeper into the feather mattress that cradled her and listened to the silence. No scraping metal spoon, no thick sole boots stomping on the wood floors, no sounds of planes and trains; just a few distant drips of water. Everyone had gone to church, and she had the house to herself.

She planned on a lazy Sunday.

Laundry. It would have to involve laundry though or otherwise tomorrow she'd be wearing shorts to work. David was lax as a boss, but not that lax.

She forced herself from the warm bed to gather the dirty clothes scattered around her room. She used to be neater than this. She wouldn't go as far as saying she was ever organized, but pre-cardboard boxes, she'd at least had a basket as a target to throw in the dirty clothes and a closet and drawers so the mess didn't lay about every surface. She searched the corners and behind the boxes for her purple sweater, but couldn't find it.

The laundry room was a screened in area off the back porch, and the rough boards were cold beneath her bare feet. She'd grown up running around these parts bare foot, and though she'd left many things behind the ten years she'd lived away, the affinity for feeling everything with her toes was not one of them.

After she sorted her clothes and was pulling knobs on the machine, she recalled that her turquoise sweater hadn't been in the stack as well. Strange.

A few days ago, some clothes had moved from the top of a box to the floor, but she hadn't thought much about it. Me'Maw may have attempted to straighten up the mess that Raleigh knew was making her unhappy. Most of the time she just kept the door closed and that was enough.

She stepped out onto the chilly back porch and was staring off at the old cypress barn when the funny feeling that was nagging her cleared. Madison had had on one of Raleigh's shirts last night.

She'd bet she'd find her clothes in Madison's room. She slipped on her flip-flops and trekked next door to her parent's house. Her parent's house was another old home, though not near as old as Me'Maw's. It had been built when dark wood paneling was the fashionable decorating choice and her parents had never updated. If you didn't flip the light switch on by the front door, you might as well jump into the swamp expecting to find your way out.

Fumbling toward the back utility room, a noise from the kitchen startled her. She'd assumed the house would be empty. Maybe Madison had decided to come home for a change. Raleigh retraced her steps and swung the kitchen door open.

Her dad sat at the table and her mom busied herself with the coffee pot. The same brown Formica countertops and green patterned wallpaper wrapped around the room. Her father's blue, chipped coffee mug waited on the counter, and the same magnets from her childhood kept Mason's drawings on the refrigerator.

"I didn't realize you'll were back already. I came to look for some clothes I think Madison borrowed."

Mom nodded, spooning sugar into the cups while the coffee maker percolated. "I think I saw them on her bed."

"Since I'm here," Raleigh cringed. Discussions with her parents had a history of going poorly. She exhaled slowly, told herself that she was a grownup, dammit, and spit it out. "Me'Maw and Paw are having a difficult time paying Madison's house note. I've offered to help, but they don't want to take it from me. I thought maybe you could help until Madison is able to do it again."

"Your grandparents are paying for the house?" Her father asked. His voice gave away his surprise, but there was a hint of something Raleigh couldn't identify.

"I know it's tough on them," her mom's eyes darted to her father, and then returned to staring at the dark liquid filling the coffee pot. Raleigh gathered that she'd known, but hadn't shared that piece of information. "But we're already paying Madison's car note and helping out with day care so she can afford it."

Raleigh reeled. "So she's not even paying for her car?"

Raleigh had bought a car last month, a fairly used car that she could afford with no help. Madison was driving around in the latest model. Raleigh had assumed she'd received insurance money for her other car, which had drowned in the bayou.

"Well, it's been slow at work, and she's had to pay off other bills."

Slow at work? Madison couldn't seem to make it to work. Raleigh had filled in so many events; she had to wonder if Madison even received a paycheck. Didn't seem like she needed one with everyone so willing to pay her bills. No, no bitterness there. Right.

"You knew that mom and dad were paying the note?" her father addressed her mother with the same questionable tone.

It was time to plan an escape route. Her father's tone reminded her of when they were teenagers and in really big trouble.

"I'll just go grab the clothes so I can finish laundry."

Her mother's perturbed, one-eyebrow-raised look followed her all the way out the door. For once, she was innocent. How was she supposed to know her mother was in on all of this?

Raleigh walked back to Me'Maw's back porch with her

arms full of her clothes. Madison hadn't asked to borrow any of the items she'd found tossed on her bed in a way that indicated her sister was familiar with her laundry routine. She'd probably planned to have them back today, or worse, send Mom with them since Mom had known where they were. Madison was six years younger, so the stealing clothes from the closet hadn't happened growing up. This must be what that was about.

She had stepped onto the back porch before she noticed Joey standing with his hands on his hips, staring at Paw's field. He wasn't in his uniform, which was a good sign. In his jeans and flannel jacket, he looked more like the cousin from Christmas dinners, than the officer that brought more trouble.

"Morning, Raleigh." Joey grinned her way, his small eyes friendly. "I was hoping to find you here. Real quiet this morning."

Raleigh headed toward the screened in utility room. It struck her then that Joey had known she'd be home alone on Sunday morning. "I suspect everyone on this street is at church. Come on in." She held the screen door open for him.

She dropped the clothes on top of the small counter and started stuffing them into the water. "What can I do for you this morning?"

She might as well get this over with. Bad news needed to be told as quickly as pulling a band-aid. At least that's what Paw always said.

"Well, now, I've come about Madison," he reached and took his work ball cap off his head. "I wanted to be discreet."

Raleigh tossed her purple sweater in and focused on him. Madison, discreet? If Madison knew what that word meant, half of Raleigh's troubles would disappear.

Joey's eyes focused on the old cane knife hanging on the weathered wood wall of the outdoor room. "It would seem before Madison was abducted, she hosted these... parties." There was a slight color that rose in Joey's cheeks. She could imagine the courage he'd had to build to come and have this conversation. Raleigh pitied him for being the only male cousin of a bunch of crazy females. "Several witnesses have come forth, and well, it appears they are waiting for her to host another one before they charge her with prostitution."

So it wasn't new trouble. Just old trouble that wouldn't go away. Raleigh had a feeling there was new trouble too, just nobody knew about it yet.

"Will they be watching her?"

Joey nodded. "Two weeks surveillance. I doubt it continues after that with money and the witnesses being a little shady and all. But I'd hate for Me'Maw and Paw to hear about any of it."

Raleigh sighed. "I'll warn Madison, but she's not listening much to me right now. I'm not sure what her problem is."

"Madison and Claudia always were wild ones. Nothing to do about it but hope she grows out of it, I suppose," Joey said, leaning against the door jam. "I'm glad you've decided to stay though. Does Me'Maw and Paw good to have you taking care of things. You just may set an example for Madison too when she decides to pay attention."

"I used to be called the trouble maker of the family. It's a sad day when the family crazy is the one who should be setting the example." Raleigh laughed.

Joey grinned. "There are different kinds of crazy. Yours ain't so bad."

Raleigh watched him ramble back to his old black Ford pickup and was contemplating walking Paw's field barefoot as she'd done as a girl when her cell phone buzzed in her pocket.

The Barbeaux's Gazette's number appeared on the screen. For a weekend off, she hadn't spent much time off.

David's far away voice greeted her. He'd put her on speakerphone. Not usually a good sign. "Mike was supposed to cover the annual church's snow day today, but I don't think it's a good idea to have him out and about covering a family event when he's under suspicion."

Raleigh groaned. She hated covering these community events. She could have written the story the first year they were held, and then change the dates and names each year and be done with it. But David was right. Mike would be lucky to make it out alive. "Okay, but Mike is going to owe me."

She could hear paper crumpling in the background. "He said this is pay back for getting him involved."

So maybe she had drug him down to find Kayla's dead body, but she didn't recall him asking her advice before he dated the loony. Maybe if he asked her for advice with women, he might actually have a girlfriend.

But, who took advice these days? No one she knew.

Eleven

Snow day at Nativity Church was like throwing ice into a muddy field and expecting more than the mud to stick. The ice melted quickly under the sweltering sun and the dirt became the consistency of sticky goo. The snow machines pumped new snow onto the hovel, and the whole thing would be a muddy mess before the four-hour festival was done. But even with the mess, the church held snow day every year in an attempt to expose the young children to snow, which in South Louisiana was as likely to fall from the sky as money. Raleigh wouldn't be surprised if the children believed that snow only came from machines. She had when she was a girl.

Raleigh weaved through the families crowding the small backyard of the church between the tombstones and the church office. The fifty-by-fifty snow pile was lined on each side by carnival booth style games. At the edge of a blue cakewalk tent, she spotted Me'Maw and Paw in a sitting area for what must have been the over 80 set. Raleigh scanned the square snowfield and spotted Mason's tangerine snow hat bobbing up and down. Madison wasn't among the sideline faces.

Raleigh spotted Thomas Roulet near the snow machine. She waved to Me'Maw and Paw as she approached Roulet, who put the event together every year. As a church volunteer, he endured the stress of the event for no pay. Raleigh knew that everyone tried to tell him how to do it every year, but they didn't help with the actual work of the festival when it came time to carry out their great ideas.

Roulet sputtered out the general sweeping statements she'd expected in a story of this nature. She could have pulled last year's story and changed the number of people who came out to celebrate and no one would have noticed. She was wrapping things up when she saw Jeffery Zedeaux walking her way.

He was the last person who'd make time to see her, so she told Mr. Roulet thank you and was writing down his last comment about the forty volunteers, when Jeffrey stepped in front of her. She looked up into a furrowed forehead and dark and stormy eyes. If it were looks alone, Jeffrey Zedeaux was a handsome man, but his personality was nasty.

"I didn't believe I could think any less of you until today." Jeffery's hands went to his hips, wrinkling his deep blue cotton shirt. His khaki pants and loafers were as dressed down as she'd seen him.

Raleigh smiled at Mr. Roulet, who nodded and went back to the snow machine. Raleigh pivoted and walked back toward the carnival games, but Jeffrey followed. What had him all worked up now? "I haven't been awake long enough to cause trouble, so I have no idea what you have decided I've done."

"How selfish can you be?" He said, yanking her arm to stop her. She whipped around and glared at him. She recognized his high school basketball court temper.

"Why don't you tell me how selfish I am then, but only after you take your hands off of me."

"It's one thing to put the financial burden of your son on Madison, but to let your aging grandparents be the ones to take care of him? That's just low even for you."

She must have missed something in the story. "Son?"

"Yes, the son you shamefully have passed off as Madison's. I can't believe you two are sisters. She is more compassionate than you have ever been."

Raleigh gaped at him. What the hell was he talking about and where was he getting his information?

"That's what I thought," Jeffrey smirked. "You can't even defend yourself. Just so you know, I'm not going to go along with this monstrosity anymore. Everyone should know what kind of person you are."

He strolled away, waving to everyone as if he was running for public office. This had Madison written all over it.

Raleigh scanned the crowd. Madison had made plans to bring Mason to this event weeks ago. Had she blown this off too?

The head of spikey dirty blonde hair towering over the crowd caught her attention. Beneath the hair were Glenn's sharp brown eyes and thick eyebrows. Glenn's hands were in his wind jacket pockets and his familiar green polo shirt peeked out of the top. He strutted through the crowd as if he'd strolled amongst Barbeaux's residents his entire life.

Her heart leapt forward and pounded in her ears. She ducked behind a hot chocolate booth near her, and watched him stroll through the milling crowd as if he'd been there his entire life. As if he belonged here. With shaking hands, she dialed Max's number and waited, trying to remember to breath.

He sounded distracted as he gave a gruff greeting.

"Max, I'm at Snow Day, and I just saw Glenn walking around."

Her voice had shook. Damn.

Silence greeted her. The trembling grew in her fingertips. "Okay, I have an officer there, but I will need you to engage him in conversation so the officer will know who he is."

"Are you crazy?" her voice squeaked. "I left in the middle of the night so I didn't have to face him."

"You can do this Raleigh Lynn." His voice was warm and reassuring. Some of the shaking in her knees subsided. The only one who called her Raleigh Lynn was Paw, and it had the same effect.

"I don't think I can."

"He can't be as scary as finding a dead body," he said.

She could hear things clinking together. "Besides, if we can take him in, you won't run into him again."

She couldn't argue with the second part. She'd prefer not to worry about him showing up everywhere she went. As far as the first reason, Raleigh rather thought the dead might not be as nerve racking.

She gritted her teeth. "That officer better hurry."

She hung up, straightened her posture, and stepped out of her hiding spot with a shudder. She felt as if she was walking into her own grave.

She caught the glint in his brown eyes the moment he spotted her. His thin lips broke into a grin visible above his four-day stubble, but it never reached his eyes. She shuddered. His intenseness had always frightened her, even when they were together. She'd mistaken it for passion then.

His large gait closed the distance between them not giving Raleigh enough time to prepare. Who was she kidding? She could have had the rest of her life and not have had time to prepare.

"I've been looking all over for you," He stepped too close to her. She could smell the overpowering astringent sting of his soap.

Her lips moved, but no sound came out of her chest, which was tight and constricted.

"I've looked for three days. Do you know how many Cheramies live in Barbeaux Bayou? What am I talking about? Of course, you do." He paused in his excited rambling to look down at her. He lunged toward her, and she only had time to tense before she couldn't breathe enclosed in his bear hug. "God, I've missed you so much."

She felt his arms around her, but stood there in stunned silence. When feeling returned enough for her to feel his hand on the small of her back, she jerked back.

The light flickered in his steely eyes, but the grin

remained.

Officer Nick appeared to her right. He looked straight at Glenn as he rested his hand on his gun holster. "I have a few questions for you, if you'd just come with me."

Raleigh looked from Glenn to Nick as she stepped back.

"No, Raleigh," Glenn protested. "I haven't done anything, I swear. I don't even know what he wants. He has the wrong person."

Raleigh stepped further back into the crowd, feeling elbows and soft body parts bang against her.

Nick stepped between them, and Glenn's tormented eyes couldn't meet her own anymore. She escaped into the crowd, walking aimlessly in whatever direction they steered her.

She bumped hard into someone, and rubbed her shoulder where it ached from contact. Raleigh focused in on who stood before her though it took effort.

"What are you doing?" Madison asked. Raleigh stared at the too low cut black top that hugged every non-curve that Madison had. Madison was pretty with her long black hair, perfectly arched eyebrows, and the confidence she carried herself with, but she could cover up a little more. That cleavage spoke volumes.

"What happened?"

"Glenn." Raleigh looked back. She couldn't see him anymore. Smiling faces strolled around them but none of them had Glenn's acorn eyes above the smiles.

Madison scanned the crowd; then guided her by her arm away from the tents. "Let's go for a walk."

A few minutes later, feeling had returned to Raleigh's limbs and complete thoughts began to form. She'd imagined that moment differently. She thought she'd be able to express her anger when she'd confronted him for the first time. Seven months had passed, but she still felt the pain of disappointment and fear.

Raleigh shook herself. She needed to stop thinking about him. The police would make sure he didn't pop up anywhere again. What she needed was to change the subject and her thoughts.

"Why does Jeffrey Zedeaux believe I'm Mason's mom?"

"He does? I have no idea." Madison scanned the crowd, not looking at her eyes.

Raleigh studied her. From her lack of eye contact, she knew that Madison knew the answer to that question. But Raleigh also knew that if she pushed it, they would have another argument. Raleigh's brain was too tired to argue. She'd leave it for later, when they weren't in public. There'd been enough of a scene today with Glenn.

"Joey stopped by earlier to warn us that a detective is looking into the parties you had. You are under surveillance for at least the next two weeks."

"Surveillance, huh?" Madison frowned. "That puts a kink in my business plans."

Raleigh stopped mid step. "Is that what you've been doing? Planning to go back in business?"

"It's good money," Madison shrugged. "Claudia and I split ten grand a month."

"But you have a job," Raleigh stammered. "One that's legal."

Madison grimaced. "A job that is going nowhere and pays little more than minimum wage. Same as you."

"I love my job, and I can afford what I want," Raleigh protested.

Madison's lips puckered in her I know more than you expression. "You're still living at Me'Maw's. It can't pay that well."

"But you were selling sex and drugs which could lead to prison."

Madison shrugged again. "I wouldn't be broke now, would I?"

The only rational explanation she had was that her sister had lost her mind. Either that or she was adopted.

Twelve

The salmon, rundown walls of Old Man Phil's bar gave no indication to the well-run establishment on the inside. The inside was old stained wood, frigid air, and a bar top that went from one end of the bayou side bar to the other. The bartender was on a first name basis with Uncle Camille and usually catered to a blue-collar work crowd, but Kayla had been here Thursday night when she was still alive, at least according to Ben from the boucherie.

She hadn't had to yank Uncle Camille out of here in the last few weeks, mainly because he hadn't felt well and couldn't walk the short distance from Cheramie Lane, so she hadn't spoken to Phil, the bartender, either.

"I was at work, Raleigh," Phil said, pulling bottles out of a crate and stacking them into a cooler behind. "But like I told the police, Thursday nights are so busy. I didn't notice who she was talking to."

Mike nodded. He'd been checking out the joint, probably trying to figure out how he managed to keep the inside nice when the outside looked like a strong wind would blow it down.

Raleigh thought a moment. "What about just telling us who was here that night that you remember?"

He nodded, pausing in his stacking. "Well, that I could probably do. Funny that detective didn't ask that."

Because they weren't really looking for the killer since they thought they already knew who he was. She didn't say that out loud though.

Mike's fingers twitched on his notepad. He took notes for everything. She was surprised that he didn't write in his sleep.

"For starters," he said, "Madison was here with Kayla for awhile. That girl Winter too."

Raleigh hoped the worry didn't show in her face.

Madison had requested an alibi for that night. Could this be why?

"Skip had come in earlier. I was glad they didn't argue as they'd done a few months ago. Kayla's sister stopped by with someone who wasn't a regular that I couldn't tell you."

"Anyone else not a regular here that night?" Raleigh asked as Mike printed the names in columns.

"I'd seen everyone at least once or twice," he shrugged.

"Was Kayla dating anyone that was a regular?"

"Nah," he said. "But awhile back she'd dated Hunter Ladeaux and he was here that night."

"Anyone else you remember?" Mike asked, looking up from his notepad.

"Nah," he shook his head. "The guys from Zedeaux shipyard were here, but they kept to themselves at the big table."

"If you hear anything from anyone, give us a call," Raleigh said, handing him a Barbeaux Gazette card.

The light blinded her as she stepped outside from the darkened bar.

"I didn't know Madison and Kayla were friends."

"Neither did I." Raleigh rubbed her scar. That's what had her worried. Madison was up to something, and although Raleigh didn't believe it was murder, she didn't want her mixed up in the investigation either. Kayla and Madison had less than a two-year age difference. Maybe they'd been friends in high school? Raleigh hadn't heard anything about a friendship in the last two months though.

Three minutes later they pulled into Me'Maw's drive and Max pulled in right behind them.

Max's hair was slicked back and it contrasted sharply with the pale blue-collar shirt. His badge on his belt loop told her he'd worked all day. Something fluttered inside her chest. She didn't have an inkling if the flutter was good or bad.

"Did you question Glenn?"

She didn't expect an outright confession, but giving the police another suspect would lessen her worry over Detective Blanch trying to prove Mike did it.

Max shook his head. "He was out in under an hour. He's very knowledgeable of the system for a construction foreman."

Her heart skipped a beat. "So he's out already?"

Max grimaced and nodded. "We had nothing and he knew it. We don't have a crime scene, only a body dump. There's no evidence to hold him. It's the same reason Will hasn't arrested Mike."

Mike's hands rubbed his neck, which he did when he was thinking. "Seems to me we need to find the crime scene if we're going to prove anything."

Max nodded without a word. Raleigh had noticed that Max didn't say much directed toward Mike these days. She tried to remember if it had been like this the last time they'd worked a case together, but she didn't think it had. She didn't like those implications.

"What if we could find the crime scene?"

Max's eyebrow rose in interest, but Mike tilted his head with caution. In that moment she realized that she was too in tune with how these two men felt. It couldn't be healthy.

Raleigh looked away from both of them. Time she spent more time in her own head. "If I went back to the barn, I could maybe connect to that moment again. I may have missed something."

"You could do that?" Max asked.

Mike looked from him to her, a frown twitching on his lips. "It doesn't work that way, Ree."

"Not usually," Raleigh said, aware that the tension had

elevated. Max was regarding Mike with the look he reserved for criminals. Far too suspicious for Raleigh's comfort. "But I also don't usually connect to them a day after their death either."

Mike shrugged, and his eyes slid away from hers. He didn't like it. She didn't need to tell him it was his name she was trying to clear. He wouldn't like it even then, though Max must think he didn't want her to do it for different reasons. It's not as if she enjoyed connecting to anyone dead or dying, but she wanted the real murderer investigated, not the ones close to her.

"Okay, then," Max said, taking a few steps backwards, his thoughts far. "If we're going to do this, we're going to do this right. I'm going to make arrangements for a witness and Will. We don't want any questions."

"What if she can't connect though?" Mike asked, leaning against the front porch.

Max had turned and was walking toward his Caprice. "I'd rather be safe than sorry. I'll call you as soon as I get everyone together."

Raleigh watched him leave and Mike remained quiet.

"I noticed you didn't mention what we learned at the bar."

Raleigh walked over and leaned against the porch next to her. "I think Madison is up to something, and I'd like to know what it is before she's implicated as a suspect."

"Up to something, huh." Mike pulled a blade of grass from the ground and twisted in his fingers. Raleigh felt it die, like a small prick echoing in her head. "Not surprising where she's concerned, but I thought she'd try harder to turn things around."

"She seems obsessed with money," Raleigh grumbled. "Says that I'll never be able to live on my own at this job."

"I do okay." Mike shrugged. "I work extra hours in

construction with Jeff to have extra cash, but you have to love what you do too."

"I think Madison loves to get in trouble and make money while doing it."

Mike elbowed her gently. He may have learned to watch the soft spots. "Maybe big sister needs to let her learn her lesson."

Raleigh grinned. "The concept is harder to see though than admit."

Mike chuckled. "I can see that."

"Let's go see if Me'Maw has some advice."

Mike nodded. "Just so you know, I know why you are doing this. Thanks."

Twenty minutes later, Mike didn't sound as if he understood. He and Me'Maw discussed her across the table as if she weren't standing there folding laundry baskets of clothes.

Mike leaned back in the old chair. Something she'd watched him do since they were teenagers. "The police haven't supported Ree before, and I don't want this to lead to more trouble for her."

Me'Maw cleared her throat. "She'll be fine. Things have a way of working out when you help others."

"I hope so, Me'Maw," Mike said, staring into space. "I don't trust it though."

Raleigh shook her head as she folded another sweater. She may as well not have been in the room as they'd discussed her for the last ten minutes without so much as asking what she thought. Mike's worries, though she knew she would ignore, were realistic. The Barbeaux police department had never given her an easy time, and this wasn't likely to make them suddenly support her.

A pain pierced the center of her forehead, and she had to close her eyes to the light that flooded her vision. It left as quickly as it had come.

The whole attempt was unconventional, but she had done it once before. She hadn't been trying then, but it had happened nonetheless. This connection had come post death, and that had her stumped. It was an unusual sequence of events, and unusual worried her. Why had it been after the death? She didn't speak to ghosts even though Me'Maw said that her great grandmother had done that too. Was that what had happened? Ghosts. Raleigh shuddered. Could she pretend that didn't happen?

She leaned over and picked the basket up when a sharp pain pierced her head, sending shock waves of pain paralyzing her body. She dropped the basket as she was overcome in darkness. Her hands gripped her head, yanking at her hair against the pain.

She pitched forward, her center of gravity lost, and as she fell, she brushed against the worn white boards of Ms. Margaret's swing.

She sank to the floor, clutching her head. Her breaths came in sharp, aching bursts.

"Pa... Paw..." she yelled, nausea shook her insides that still clinched with the pain.

Within moments, his heavy boots stomped across the porch and the screen door creaked open as he yanked it hard.

She kneaded her temples, feeling a small burst in her head.

"Ms. Margaret," she gulped. Pain meant she was still alive. She swayed between this knowledge and the desire for the pain to go away. "Ms. Margaret...stroke... swing...."

The chair beneath Mike scraped against the floor as he sprang forward.

"Ma, call for an ambulance," Paw said before stomping off, limping on his aching arthritis legs after Mike.

Me'Maw reached for the phone while Raleigh rocked back and forth, telling herself pain was good. Pain meant life. She was afraid she didn't mean it enough because she yearned for it to stop.

The screen door creaked again.

"What's going on? I saw dad running to the front?"

Her dad stood in the doorway and looked down at her on the floor as if he'd never seen someone sitting in the center of a floor. Like she didn't end up on her butt often these days.

Me'Maw clutched the phone to her chest but sank back into her chair. Me'Maw closed her eyes. "Margaret just had a stroke."

"Oh." he stared at them. The wheels turned, but he was getting there slowly. Finally, he crossed to Raleigh and reached out and helped her up from the floor. She sank into the chair across from Me'Maw.

He brought her a water bottle from the fridge, and then stood in the middle of the kitchen in blue Dickie pants like his father. The men in Raleigh's life were all the strong, silent type who wanted to come to the rescue but had no idea what to do. Instead, the women in the family had to come to the rescue time and time again.

"Why don't you go check on Paw?" Raleigh said placing the cold bottle to her forehead. It eased some of the heat throbbing through her head.

He nodded himself out the back door. The pain still resided in her skull, but it had receded to the sides instead of straight through the center. Did that mean Ms. Margaret was leaving slowly or that she wasn't dying?

Where was that instruction manual again? She glanced over at Me'Maw's hands fiddling with the cards. She stared into space, but the shuffling of the cards was deliberate and rhythmic.

During the pause of the shuffling, Raleigh reached across and pulled a card from the stack and lay it face down on the table. The two of spades stared up at them.

Me'Ma's chest heaved and her shoulders slumped. Raleigh's eyes watered and her chest compressed.

Thirteen

Footsteps thundered up on the back porch steps, Mike's pale face appeared through the swinging screen door.

"She's still alive." He grimaced. "The ambulance just left with her, and Paw and your dad are calling her son."

Raleigh's insides clinched. She eased the card back into the pile and shook her head. Ms. Margaret would live only a few days.

He exhaled, and it filled the room, but then the chair scratched against the wooden floor and he sank into it next to her at the table.

Silence set in around the table. For the millionth time, she thought how she'd much rather have Me'Maw's talent. Death exhausted her down through her bones.

The shrill ringtone of her cellphone interrupted the silence.

"Raleigh," Max barked into the phone. She could tell he was walking outside from the far away sound to his voice. "I'm ready for you down at the crime scene. All arrangements are made."

"Okay." Her brain was weary and slow. It took a moment for her to remember she was to go to the crime scene. She couldn't do this. She opened her mouth to protest but by that time the dial tone sounded in her ear.

"I don't think I can do this," she said, looking up at Mike.

"They're ready?"

Raleigh nodded.

"Listen here, Raleigh Lynn," Me'Maw's stooped shoulders pulled up some. "Margaret was ninety-one years old, and if there is such a thing, it was her time. That young woman had her life taken, and it wasn't God's hands that did the taking. You need to help make it right if you can. That's all He asks of you, of any of us."

Raleigh looked into the crinkled blue eyes that were soft and warm. Me'Maw's faith was unshakeable. How did she never give up? The living offered their fair share of bad things, and she believed with her big heart that it was all going to work out.

Mike shrugged and held his hand out to her. "All we can do is try."

That's all they could do. That, and eat plenty of chocolate to ease the sadness. A good coping mechanism that hadn't failed her yet. She may have to eat it by the pound at times, but it worked.

They stopped at a gas station on the way to Dantin Farm. While Mike ran inside, Raleigh watched an argument between a man and a woman outside. She couldn't hear the words through the heavy plastic windows, but the look on the girl's face was pure rage. The guy had his hands tucked in his pockets with sinking shoulders. They looked young, maybe early twenties. His LSU sweatshirt had seen better days, and her fur boots were slung over jeans with slashes down the front. She gestured wildly about, and he slunk further away from her. Raleigh didn't know what he'd done, but unless he'd lost their first-born child in a gambling bet, it wasn't worth it.

A slight sting from him shuddered through her. It had been a strange popping sound. Quick and final. Had she just felt love die?

Everything died. This she knew, but why would she be able to feel love die? The thought sent a shiver through her. That could be problematic living in an area where love died as quickly as you could give a second look to the delivery man or your friend's husband.

Mike hopped into his seat and tossed a brown paper bag onto the dashboard. She was being silly and a bit morbid. Why would she think she could feel love die? It must have been her imagination. The reassurance didn't reach through the sadness settling into her chest. Death was settling in.

At the Dantin property, Max's Caprice was parked near a navy blue town car. They parked near Nate's old barn just as the sun was falling behind the clouds. The yellow crime scene tape flapped against the old cypress boards, and several cows grazed beyond a barbwire fence.

As Raleigh stepped out of the car, the chilly December air ripped at her cheeks. It had been colder the last time they'd been out here. She'd had her nerves to warm her up then though.

Max approached, but Raleigh squinted at the pretty blonde from the station now leaning against the hood of Max's car and Detective Blanch glaring at them from near the shallow grave with his arms crossed. Couldn't Max maybe have brought witnesses that liked her? He should have been able to find at least one around the station.

Max nodded curtly to Mike. "The scene is clear so you can touch anything."

Raleigh scanned the open pasture. The long grass fluttered in the breeze, but the remoteness of the area created a calming silence. Three cows grazed under a group of trees about five hundred feet back, but otherwise no one else was around. The other night she hadn't been able to see how remote the area was. She'd come here in high school only when there'd been a party and the emptiness hadn't been relevant then since it had been one giant parking lot.

Max looked to her, his intense gaze focused solely on her. It always warmed her as if he could see all of her doubts and fears through her eyes. Could he see the fear that clouded her thoughts now? Had she been crazy to volunteer for this? Yes. "How do you want to do this?"

Raleigh shrugged, looking away from him. "I just need quiet."

Her heart pounded harder with each step toward the grave.

Whoever had dug the hole, had piled it on the left. It didn't really qualify as a pile as it didn't add up to much. The killer had barely dug a foot into the ground. Had he or she been scared off or had the intention been for her to be found? Her thoughts returned to the stillness of the area. No one would have come back here at night to disturb the burial.

She made a wide sweeping circle around the shallow hole. She could feel the internal tight rope balance with each careful step she took. She wanted to know what had happened to Kayla but her insides trembled with the thought of reaching out and connecting.

Why had she thought she could do this? Two months ago her cousin's murder scene had been a fluke. She connected to people as they died. That's how she liked it: simple and predictable. If she had to be abnormal, she'd like for it to be done in the usual way.

Kayla's death had been unusual from the beginning, she muttered to herself.

"This is a waste of time." Detective Will Blanch's booming voice jarred her out of her deep thoughts.

"I agree," The woman called. Her flowered skirt fluttered with the wind. Who dressed up to go to a crime scene?

Someone trying to impress someone; that's who.

The silence of the area crowded her ears. No animals fluttered in the chilled air; no frogs croaked. She'd asked for silence, and the critters had granted it to her. Raleigh stopped circling the grave. She approached Max and Mike standing a few feet from each other in silence. She couldn't connect if her thoughts were on whether Max had a thing for blondes now. Why was this woman here again?

Mike set his brown bag down on Max's hood next to a box of Apple Tree doughnuts. Several Twix peeked out of the bag and Raleigh snatched one up. Max's expression hardened.

He must have bought the doughnuts, knowing her blood pumped with sugary treats. The slight twinge of guilt she felt didn't overcome the gratification of a Twix right now. Max still had much to learn.

"My mind is rejecting it," she said, nibbling on her lip to appease her polite southern manners requirement before tasting the dose of chocolate her body yearend for.

"It's okay," Max said, looking over the empty pasture to hide the disappointment his voice hinted at.

The grave looked out of place in the grassy pasture. Someone had hid her here, but hadn't even cared enough to do it right. They'd tossed her in a shallow grave, thrown a few shovels of dirt over her like a blanket, and gone home to their life. The beauty of the dilapidated barn with its hale bales and old tractor equipment peeking out had been tainted. It was a shadow that lurked in the otherwise pristine setting.

"It's not right," Raleigh said, ripping open the package with her frustration.

"Maybe you're looking at it the wrong way," Mike said, looking at her with his big green, sympathetic eyes. He knew how difficult this was for her. "You don't need to see her death; only where she was. Focus on that."

Raleigh nodded, playing with the idea. Not seeing actual death held appeal. Her brain had tired of death, and it made her feel vulnerable to open up so soon. To catch a glimpse of the location would take away the pressure of opening herself completely again.

"I think I can do that."

"Oh please," The woman groaned, a thin frown twitching at her rose petal lips. "As if any of this is real. We'll never find out what happened to my sister this way."

Sister? Interesting. Old man Phil had said that the sister was at the bar Thursday night. She may want to be involved in an investigation if she knew she'd done something. Raleigh stole a glance at Max, whose gaze remained far off on the field. Was she a suspect or was she helping him as Raleigh had done only two months ago?

"I agree this is a waste of time," Detective Blanch said, shifting his stance. "If she knows anything, she'd protect that one anyway." He pointed toward Mike. Raleigh stiffened. Why did everyone think she would lie to protect him? She probably would, but she hadn't yet. Give her some credit people.

"He's Ross Blanch's cousin," Max mumbled as he stepped closer toward the grave.

Well that explained the attitude and confirmed her suspicions. She'd shot Ross in self-defense in high school. The family had held it against her ever since. Understandable, but they didn't need to be jerks about it.

Raleigh bit into her Twix and strolled over to the shallow grave again. Her flesh rose on her arm as she looked down into the hole. Glossy eyes flashed before her. The eyes she'd looked into under the moonlight when she'd found the body. Raleigh closed her eyes against the lifeless image. She needed the moments before they'd glazed over, when they'd still had that light in them.

She sank down next to the hole, instinct telling her she needed to be closer for the connection.

The eyes appeared, floating above the grave. Maybe she needed the eyes. It was a trick of the eye really- death or life- just a small amount of light would indicate life. She focused on adding the light instead of pushing the eyes away.

She walked through the eyes as if they were a door.

She stumbled on the pavement. Her feet didn't feel as if they were part of her body, though the thought rattled in her head that it was silly to believe otherwise. The cement below her was cast in shadows, more darkness than light. Her heavy head rolled and took effort and concentration to look up at the one street lamp that lit the open parking lot. The light multiplied before her and she was overwhelmed with the smell of gardenia and alcohol, reminiscent of cheap perfume. Another smell burned her nose and her throat when she inhaled, but Raleigh could not place it. It was strange and herbal and unfamiliar.

The lights and cement spun topsy-turvy and she could feel her body sinking. Somewhere beyond the edges, she knew her real body was sinking into the grave, but she clung to the connection with everything in her.

She needed a place. She couldn't lose the connection or she may never get it back.

Six red doors spun before her. They came in and out of focus blending into one and then separating into six.

Another her, the one beneath the connection, felt strong hands grip her arms, but she pushed on, straining into the wavering connection. Nauseousness clinched her stomach and her body quivered. *She would not be sick.*

The red door spun in circles, but a dark spot towards the top on the door bothered her. Something stuck to the door, maybe? A number! If only it would stop being a spinning kaleidoscope.

"Raleigh!" Max's voice tunneled to her. "Raleigh!"

Weights pulled down on her shoulder, pulling her toward that red door, but she squeezed his hand.

The number on the door blurred and focused, and slowly from the red, a black number eight emerged.

But where? Where was door number eight?

She needed a landmark. Her head rolled as she sank into the body, not just the blueness of her eyes. Max and Mike's pull disappeared from her arms. A chill crawled up her bare legs, her heart raced, and her body wouldn't listen to her commands.

She was Kayla. Raleigh fought the feeling of light-headedness and sluggish movement to turn her head to see the bright green sign glowing Barbeaux Bed and Breakfast.

The red door swung open and darkness lay beyond. Raleigh's heart pounded, fear coursed through her. She'd sunk into the connection and was now stumbling into the darkness.

She wanted out before she experienced her death. Had it happened right away? Had it taken awhile?

Raleigh gasped as she fell back against the grass near the grave. Mike and Max clasped her arms so tight she could feel the bruises swelling.

Raleigh scrambled out of the hole, feeling the blue eyes gloss over into the porcelain doll.

Mike and Max helped her to her feet, and she hoped she wouldn't collapse like a matchstick on her trembling legs.

"She was at Barbeaux Bed and Breakfast," Raleigh rubbed her cheeks and then her arms. She shivered from the iciness that had crept over her. "Room eight. She was drugged."

The young woman gasped and covered her mouth with her hands. "That's not possible. She can't know that. Can she?"

She stared at them, eyes wide, bottom lip trembling. Raleigh returned her stare. No way she had relived that to have someone doubt her. Tears tumbled one by one down the sister's face and then she burst with a groan of agony.

Belief. Raleigh felt relief and pity surge through her.

Max stepped closer and put his arm around the woman's shoulder to support her shaking. She buried her face in his chest again.

More tears? Did the woman do anything else but cry? More importantly, did Max find this attractive? He offered comfort when it happened. Raleigh didn't like it one bit.

Blanch caught her eye with a sneer that twitched at his lips. "Max likes to offer comfort. Don't take it too personal. He gets close for a short time to everyone we work with."

Raleigh hated him more in that moment than she had when he was interrogating her. Maybe what she should be investigating was whether his statement was true.

Fourteen

The loud buzzing caused Raleigh to cringe. After three false starts, she and Mike had tracked down Hunter Ladeaux, Kayla's ex-boyfriend. Hunter owned a yard service company, and after speaking to his secretary an hour ago, they'd followed the list of customers to the local savings and loan bank.

Another grinding of tree limbs into mulch shook her down to her teeth.

"Okay, I say we interrupt," Raleigh said, standing up from her lean to against the Jeep.

Mike nodded, and Raleigh realized that he was looking off towards the dentist office next door behind a massive oak tree. She followed his focus to find a police cruiser parked in a spot facing them. It hadn't been there when they'd pulled in five minutes ago. Dammit. Didn't they have better things to do? It's not as if Mike was going to do anything on a Monday morning in the bright daylight. Not that he'd do anything anyway. She muttered under her breath.

As they approached, the vibrating rose through her feet and she felt as if something would shake loose. Her brain couldn't handle anything else knocking around in there.

When they were near enough for Raleigh to smell the grease in the machine, Hunter finally noticed them.

"Hello, you guys," he smiled warmly. "I need you folks to keep back if you don't mind."

"Raleigh Cheramie from the Barbeaux Gazette." She stuck her hand out. "We have a few questions if you don't mind."

He nodded and reached a thick hand to the machine, and in moments, silence descended on her ears. She thought she'd gone deaf.

Hunter wasn't exactly handsome. He wasn't awful to look at, but his lips were abnormally large, his eyebrows were bushy, and his face looked larger than it should for his average height. He did have a gorgeous head of thick black hair that flopped over to one side in a lazy, careless way. It was his best feature.

"What can I do for ya'll?" He asked, leaning against the side of the machine.

"We were hoping you could tell us a little about Kayla Duncan," Mike said, glancing behind him to check the status of the police car.

It still sat in the same place.

"Oh, now," he shrugged. His shoulders were too small for his head. "I don't know much more than anyone else. I was real sad to hear about her death though. She was a nice girl."

"Phil told us that you two dated?" Raleigh asked.

He nodded. "Real interesting girl. Not sure she was ready for a relationship with the divorce and all, but I'd hoped she'd figure it all out and settle down."

And go back to him. She could see the sorrow in his acorn eyes and the frown lines around his lips. Even though she couldn't stop picturing his head as a big balloon over his body, he appeared to be a good guy.

"Was she seeing anyone now?" Mike's laid-back stance had disappeared with the police car. She could tell he was only half paying attention.

"Nahh..." Hunter looked toward the bank and the pile of tree branches still to go. "Not that I know about. Madison Cheramie may know."

"Madison?" Raleigh's flesh prickled. Why did Madison's name keep coming up? It was never a good thing to have your own sister's name come up during a murder investigation.

Hunter's black hair bobbed. "Those two had been working together on something the last few weeks."

Raleigh glanced back at that police car herself. She felt as if any moment the uniform inside was going to pounce and accuse them of hiding information important to the case.

"Do you know anything about it?"

"Naa..." he shook his head and thumped his thumb on the white machine. "Kayla only said she'd make enough money to move out of her parent's house."

He blushed and looked away. "Truth is... with everything that went around a few months ago about Madison... I really didn't want to ask."

He'd grown uncomfortable and fidgety. His words had exerted quite the effort and sweat had popped out on his forehead.

She felt as though she needed to put him out of his misery.

"If there's anything else you remember or hear, please let us know." Raleigh handed him a card.

She and Mike made polite good-byes and then headed back toward the Jeep.

Mike swept the area with his eyes. "I hate to say this but Madison seems all over this."

Raleigh nodded. "Can you imagine how it will go when we question her?"

Mike grimaced. "We need more before we go to her. Something she can't deny so she has to tell us how she's involved."

Raleigh nodded. A few months ago when Max had accused her sister, she'd furiously jumped all over him. She knew Mike didn't mean that Madison had murdered Kayla. He knew Madison just as well as Raleigh knew her. Which meant they both knew that Madison could get herself tangled in a mess that was as difficult to get out of as a crab trap. Unfortunately, Madison was just as furious as that crab that had been caught in that trap, unwilling to let anyone help.

The sad blue shotgun house was just as Raleigh expected it with its neighbors able to have a conversation standing in front of an open window. Two hours ago, she'd been twirling in her chair at work, only to be interrupted by Me'Maw who'd needed a favor. Her Southern manners didn't allow refusing her grandmother anything, so she was now down Pine Street at the family home of an old friend. The street spoke volumes for its residents. Sadly, it had not improved what it said about the people who lived here in the last few years.

"You remember what Me'Maw said?" Paw asked, easing his old truck into a driveway with more deep holes than shells

Raleigh nodded. "It will be fine."

What Me'Maw had told her caused more than a little quibble. Raleigh hoped she didn't have to resort to lying, and she had to wonder if Me'Maw had ever done it to any of the many people who traveled, some great distances, to see her.

This old friend was a grieving mother whose son had died in a tragic motorcycle accident. Raleigh was to assure the family that he'd gone peacefully no matter what impression she received that said otherwise.

Raleigh had protested because she didn't reassure the living. She saw death and gave the dead peace. Besides, yesterday's connection had left her head a little fuzzy and concentration had come and gone all day. She'd dumped Mike's coffee over on his desk, emailed the wrong story-- twice, and dropped her Twix into the trash instead of the wrapper. Even her Mondays weren't typically that bad.

She'd had enough of the dead for a while-- thank-you very much.

But refusing Me'Maw or Paw wasn't an option.

Raleigh sighed and pulled on the door handle to get out the truck. She dreaded having to reassure the mother that her son Blade (After a knife, really?) had left this world and gone to heaven instead of linger as a ghost about the house.

The grass reached her shins, and she had to brace herself as she waded through it. She hoped it was only grass brushing against her legs. A chill ran up the back of her neck. She hated bugs, and the grass felt like bugs crawling over her.

Paw walked ahead of her and knocked with a short rap on the front screen door. A deep "come in" came from inside, and Paw swung the door open without hesitation.

The smell of dog urine, sweat, and Tabaco filled her nostrils, throat, and lungs on first step. She clinched her leg muscles to prevent herself from physically turning around. She would have taken a much deeper breath outside if she had known about the stench on the other side of that screen door.

Ms. Zola sank into her old brown farm patterned sofa with the expression of a woman who'd been beaten and given up. A decade ago she'd looked younger than Raleigh's parents. Today she appeared Ms. Margaret's age with her black bags under her eyes and her drooping flesh on her face.

A younger woman in a bright orange tank top three sizes too small for her hefty chest size leaned forward in a country blue recliner. Black mascara was smeared down her right eye and her tangled hair hadn't seen a brush in a few days. The house must not have any mirrors.

"I brought my girl, Ms. Zola, Ms. Terrie," Paw said, nodding his head to each of them.

"Thank you so much, Will," Ms. Zola said, her lip quivering as she spoke. "It will do us so much good. I just know it will."

"It don't matter," Terrie rasped. "Nothing matter anymore. My boy's gone."

"Don't talk like that, Terrie," Zola snapped. "It matters to Blade where he's at. He matters. Go on sweetheart. We won't be disturbing you."

Raleigh returned Terrie's leery look. Terrie didn't quite wear the expression of someone who'd given up. She looked more like the type who'd hit first and brag about it later. But it may have been those pink scars that looked like finger nails across her chest that was speaking to Raleigh.

No more favors. The only requests she'd be taking from now on would be the dead. The living could get scary.

Raleigh moved around the ten-by-ten living area just to do something. She hadn't seen a dog yet, but she certainly smelled its presence. From a cheap wooden shelf by a doorway, a few picture frames stared at her.

She picked up a framed picture of a young twenty year old posing on a street bike. He smiled in the picture though his eyebrows and face appeared to glare in annoyance at the photographer. He was wearing a black muscle shirt, and a superman tattoo with a ring of barbwire was plastered on his forearm.

Raleigh's head felt fuzzy and the overwhelming stench of this place wasn't making clarity easy.

She put the picture back down on the shelf and closed her eyes

She didn't want to lie, but she didn't want to connect either. She didn't even like that it might work this way. It meant that there was a new normal, and she didn't want a new normal. What was wrong with the old way? Nothing felt normal these days.

On the next shelf, Blade leaned against an old beat up blue Camaro. In this picture he looked older. His hair was thinner, shorter and the tattoo ink lighter. The facial expression remained the same though, a thin growl in his eyes but a forced smile on his lips.

Raleigh brushed her finger against the picture. She could just say it as she'd rehearsed it in her head and leave; be done with this tired, gloomy home.

It wasn't right though. The words wouldn't rise above the lump in her throat. What if it wasn't true? Didn't Blade deserve peace, not just his family?

She moved on to a scratched and scoffed end table where a picture was face down on its surface. Raleigh turned it over, for the first time feeling the eyes of everyone else in the room on her. She looked at the wreckage of the Camaro, her fingers bleeding into the edges of the blue line, and she slid into the car instantly.

He'd gone quickly. No second thoughts. No last regrets. He'd driven the motorcycle straight into the side of the Camaro with his ex-girlfriend inside, gaping at him horrified. She'd screamed; he hadn't.

Raleigh shuddered and placed the photo back on the table, careful to face it down again.

"He went instantly," Raleigh said, her voice trembled slightly. She gathered herself. "He didn't stay behind."

"Thank goodness," Ms. Zola exclaimed. Relief lifted some of the heaviness in her face. "Praise Jesus. He didn't suffer."

Terrie dabbed at her black stained eyes with a balled up tissue. "Are you sure?"

Raleigh nodded. "I felt him leave."

Her legs began to tremble. The smell, the heat, and the fuzziness in her head threatened to overwhelm her.

"Excuse me a moment," Raleigh said, slipping out the

door in one fluid motion.

The cool outside air filled her as she took her first deep breath and the nausea eased some. She needed a longer break from death. She felt off-balance, as if she wasn't quite standing in this world completely. Was it possible to get stuck? To not be able to slip in and out as she'd been doing.

Paw's heavy boots knocked loudly on the porch behind her. "I'm ready if you are, girl." He stopped next to her and looked over at her from under his bushy eyebrows. "Are you feeling alright?"

"I haven't felt right since yesterday," she said and then noticed the concern twitch at the corners of his soft eyes. "I'll be fine. I think it was just too much at one time."

He nodded, though the concern didn't evaporate. "The family held a collection for you to do it. She said it's about $200."

He handed her the folded wad of cash, and as she took it, she looked back at the ramshackled old house. It was more money than that house had seen in a while. "Do you think we should give it back? They look like they may need it more."

Paw shook his head as he balanced himself and lumbered sideways down the steps. "You'd be insulting their pride. Take it and do something good with it."

Raleigh stared at the money in her palm. She wasn't going to lie; she didn't see extra money often. Somehow she didn't think new black boots would qualify as good according to Paw. When Paw reached the bottom step, she handed it back to him. "Then take it and put it toward the house payment. It will make me feel better." Raleigh added as he opened his mouth to protest. "I don't want the house to be sold to a stranger either."

His lips grew thin and straightened for a moment as he thought about it, but then he nodded and pocketed the money.

The drive back to the house was quiet. Paw had always been content to remain silent in his truck, just like 35 MPH was a good speed for him. It took them twice as long to reach Cheramie Lane, but the fuzziness in her head made her feel as if she wasn't in her body, so she barely noticed.

This could be normal, not that Raleigh even knew what normal felt like. But most people might be blaming a brain tumor right about now and seeking medical advice. The only advice a doctor would give her was to check into a mental hospital. Uncle Camille's training could answer some of her questions, but she'd have to get him to train her first.

Now, that was the first good idea she'd had all day.

Maybe it was time to stop being nice. Sour people didn't respond to sugar and Uncle Camille was one of those sour, bitter old men. She needed a new tactic.

Twenty minutes later she stood on Uncle Camille's porch braced for an argument. Uncle Camille sat stooped over in his usual beat up ladder-back chair near the door, but the man with the leather pouch from the other day sat on the porch leaning against a post, chewing on a long sugar cane reed. He looked at home amongst the grass that brushed the top of the porch. Raleigh had tripped over an ice chest in the middle of the yard because she couldn't see it beneath the grass. She felt anything but at home here.

"You agreed to train me. You told Me'Maw you would," Raleigh said. His five-minute rant about her not deserving the traiteur knowledge had grown old. He thought she was dark and evil and everything traiteurs worked against. Blah. Blah. Blah. She suffered her own self-doubts. She didn't need someone causing more. Besides Me'Maw and Father Lucas believed she was good, and they weren't bitter dying men.

His lips sneered and his words slurred. "Me'Maw doesn't choose, I do."

Raleigh knew the argument was useless. *Tete deur,* Paw's nickname for her, ran in the family- stubbornness was a family trait.

Dardar spoke quietly, with a slowness of rhythm measured with your heartbeat. "I say if she wants to know, she deserves to learn her heritage."

Uncle Camille's glare didn't shift, but the sneer disappeared. "This one doesn't deserve the knowledge. Madison deserves it more, and she's just a whore."

"Fine then," Raleigh said exasperated. She reminded herself that it was wrong to tackle someone in his weakened condition. Me'Maw would never forgive her. "At least explain the fuzzy feeling in my head. How do I fix it?"

"I say you should have them lock you up before you hurt anyone else. I might tell them myself; be doing everyone a favor."

Raleigh glared at him, biting down on her lip until the pain shot through her. She could feel the stench of death on him, though the odor was less assaulting today. She dug deep for some sympathy, but it wasn't bubbling to the surface. He still blamed her for his daughter's death, though technically it was Madison's fault. *Tete deur.*

She could feel Dardar's eyes on her before she looked at him. Again his voice captured her pulse. "My grandmother was a spirit walker."

Raleigh's eyebrows rose. Spirit walker? That sounded Native American, but so much cooler than Traiteur to the dead. How come Me'Maw hadn't offered that as a title? It wrapped it up in a pretty package, and these days something needed to be pretty about it.

He continued and she had to pull herself from her sluggish thoughts. "I had a cousin who was a spirit talker. At least that's my family's name for the abilities passed down through the generations. My grandmother was like you though. She walked with those who were dying, taking their journey with them."

That pretty package of a name sounded even better right now. Native American or Cajun didn't make much difference to her. She'd take advice from a squirrel right now if it would help.

"Did she ever talk about her head being fuzzy?"

Dardar shrugged, a piece of the sugar cane stalk dangling from the side of his lip. "She said there was a hole in her head where they came and went. Maybe your hole is feeling empty."

Maybe she should find that squirrel. How was that logical? People didn't have holes in their heads unless something was wrong with them... Raleigh had plenty things wrong with her but that wasn't one of them for once.

He laughed, a deep laugh from his chest. His gaze pierced through her as if he saw deep into her thoughts. "Always difficult to explain to people."

Raleigh's cheeks warmed. It was as if he could read her mind. Weeks ago she'd felt like that with Max. Now, if he could read her mind, they wouldn't be having dating issues.

"It's not a literal hole." His voice returned to the soothing lullaby. "There is a place that the dying occupies when you connect. Maybe you are getting used to them filling it, and it feels fuzzy when they are absent."

Raleigh nodded. That could be logical, right? Oh, whom was she kidding? It sounded as if she needed to check herself into that hospital.

"I feel as if everything is a little wacky." Raleigh hesitated. She'd always hated talking about it. But desperate times... "I usually only connect in the moment of death, but twice in the last week it hasn't been that way."

He nodded, tossing his sugarcane stalk into the yard where it disappeared into the tangle. Good. She'd felt its death and preferred it to be further away. "Death is death. The energy they project towards you may take an hour, a day, or a decade to reach you, but you are a spirit walker. You feel the energy released when someone dies. It doesn't have to be the exact moment."

Raleigh's inner child voice screamed, yes it did. "It always has been before."

"The space grows larger each time you open it up. Before you didn't give them much room to occupy, so they couldn't stay."

Maybe she was crazy because that sort of made sense to her. She'd connected through a photograph today. She'd never done that before. It was sort of cool in a creepy way. She'd even received payment for it. The dead couldn't pay her, but the living could, and that sounded like a way to earn extra money so that she could help out her grandparents or maybe be independent like Madison had said.

She was getting ahead of herself. That ill-conceived plan meant that she'd have to have many more connections with the dead inside her fuzzy head. Enlarging the space that they could come and go as they pleased wasn't as appealing of an idea as the extra cash.

Fifteen

Traffic slowed to a standstill. Raleigh sank further into the seat of her car. School traffic. This was why she typically went to work later, so she could avoid the frustration of being at a dead stop on a highway. Jeff wanted her and Mike in early for a meeting though, so she was caught inching toward the bridge she needed to turn left on, and not anywhere close to turning.

Sheri's Creative Images peeked out from behind an old abandoned gas station. The shop was once a home that you would have tripped over the kitchen sink when getting out of bed in the morning. Sheri managed to make it work for her clients though, and she even had a girl who did nails twice a week at a manicure table in the corner. The navy blue sedan parked out front was alone. She probably hadn't had her first appointment yet.

Raleigh tapped on the steering wheel. She hadn't dropped in on Sheri in over two weeks. Maybe what she needed in her life right now was a female's perspective. Males dominated too much of her day and thoughts, and that couldn't be good. She nudged onto the shoulder and pulled into the parking lot. It beat waiting in traffic.

The bell above the door clanged her arrival and Sheri stopped mid scrub to look up.

"Hey girl," she smiled and leaned over the sink, resting her big bosom on the edge. "Didn't expect to see you awake so early."

"Work calls," she grumbled. "But I needed some advice." She eased into the swivel chair and swished herself around. Her stomach quivered with the motion and her heart pumped a little faster. No, it never got old.

Sheri chuckled. "Well, I usually have plenty of that to go around."

"Max seems to be close to Kayla's sister." Raleigh twirled one more time for good measure, but then decided she should stop when the quiver rose up into her throat. Too much of a good thing led to regret when her head began spinning. "As in maybe he and I aren't dating exclusively and I was under the impression we were."

"Humph," Sheri said, picking up a cape from the floor, walking toward the other empty chair. "I'm not saying that it isn't an issue, but personally, I'd be worried about the dates he doesn't show up for more. At some point it becomes a bad habit, and bad habits are meant to be kicked to the curb."

Raleigh bit down on her bottom lip. Wasn't there anyone who had a different opinion? "Mike agrees with you. I thought maybe the female perspective would be different."

"I only tell you how I see it." Sheri's big shoulders lifted up in a shrug. "You two aren't dating unless you actually go out on a date."

A girl couldn't argue with logic. But she couldn't make him show up on a date, and she had enough pride not to beg. Besides, she'd like for him to want to see her enough to make an effort, work or no work. Perhaps she just needed to admit that it wasn't going to work out.

"I hate relationships," Raleigh exclaimed, spinning around again, as the queasy feeling rose in her stomach. She'd reached her limit. In more than one way.

Sheri frowned, sinking into the chair. "Tell me about it. Shawn's father is a pain in my ass."

"Oh, is he out of rehab?" Raleigh asked, standing so she didn't get any more sudden impulses to spin around. The fuzziness in her head had receded to a tolerable level, so she didn't want to risk it rising up and snapping at her.

"Next week." She furrowed her eyebrows. "His lawyer

already contacted me about his visitation. Lawyer fees make me poorer than dirt."

Sheri's ex had been through rehab seven times in the last three years. Each time Deon came out, he took her back to court for custody. Then three months later he'd forget to visit Shawn because he was too messed up to realize what day of the week it was. Each time Sheri had to pay her lawyer. Raleigh was surprised the judge would still hear from him. But then again it was Barbeaux Bayou, so he was probably related to the judge. Everyone knew everyone in small towns, which wasn't always a good thing... unless your connections were in charge.

Raleigh listened and sighed in the right places at the new terms Deon was badgering her for, before heading out five minutes later for her meeting.

When she entered the Barbeaux Gazette's newsroom, Mike was leaning back in his chair and David was standing in the small aisle between their desks and his office door. Jeff's forehead was etched with the two wrinkles he wore as often these days as his favorite alligator tie. He needed to relax before they became permanent. He may as well sign up to premature aging right now.

"I don't like this predicament." David looked off above their heads as he rocked back and forth on his feet. "It's not okay for us not to cover the investigation, but it will look bad if you two cover it."

Raleigh rocked back in her desk chair. "You will have to write the stories."

The wrinkles on his forehead deepened.

Mike coughed to hide his laughter. "Raleigh and I will do all the work, but we will use your byline on the stories. Everyone wins."

David's eyes grew distant, and he rocked back and forth on the balls of his feet. David was weighing his options and reasoning logically with himself. Sometimes, he muttered aloud his internal thoughts, but today his rationalization carried on in silence.

Mike and Raleigh's eyes met and both bit down on a grin. David the predictable.

"Okay, I think this will work," he said. "Have something on my desk today so I can go over the story and offer my opinion."

"You got it boss." Raleigh grinned, and Mike winked at her. David never surprised them, but they enjoyed letting him believe he had control.

David pivoted and faced his office door, but stopped. "And guys, let's try not to get so close next time."

Was that an option? Stumbling after the dead wasn't her idea of fun. She'd never explained the whole traiteur to the dead to him as it wasn't her favorite type of conversation. She wanted for at least a few individuals to believe she was normal, but if the dead kept making headlines, she'd have to confess.

Mike threw a baseball into the air and caught it. "How about a lunch strategy meeting to divide and conquer?"

"Sounds good," Raleigh said, pulling the notes for her parish council story. "I have dibs on interviewing the sister."

Mike grinned, as he typed into his computer. "Plan to throw any personal questions into that interview?"

"You know it." Raleigh grinned. Sheri's advice had got her thinking that if Max was dating Kayla's sister Mandy, then it was time for her to move on and stop waiting for him to show up on a date.

For lunch, they headed to their usual place, Mirv's Diner. The diner occupied the same place it had since the 1930s in the only part of Barbeaux Bayou that could be considered a downtown area. It hadn't seen any signs of revitalization, and only nine buildings were in use on the two-block area.

Once, every public office building occupied this area, including a hardware store, Mirv's Dinner, and a department store.

Today, only Mirv's remained. There was a dance studio in one building and a recently opened hardware store as well as a dentist's office. The rest were odds and ends that opened with a burst of excitement and fizzled out quickly, making room for whatever someone wanted to try next. Most remained empty.

A month ago, a bakery had opened in the space near Mirv's and rumor was that the pies were better than anything your mama made. Raleigh had heard from Darlene at the news station that Madelyn, the young twenty something year old owner, had used her grandmother's recipes to develop her selection. That, of course, garnered everyone's curiosity. Because if it was old, it had to be good. If food was a religion, the older recipes were the bible.

Mirv's tables were filled with its usual lunch crowd. Raleigh and Mike squeezed into a corner table near the old glass case of town memorabilia. The waitress's rounds took ten minutes before she reached them for their order of the white beans and fried catfish lunch special, and by the time the young brunette delivered their plates, they'd planned their interviews and divided the research.

Raleigh fiddled with her straw and scanned the diner without tilting her head up. Most tables were filled with regulars; people she saw every time she was in here. Nothing against Mirv's, but most people came here for the cheap dinner specials in a town with limited choices.

She'd begun to draw her focus back to her notepad when Madison's fluttering eyelids caught her attention. Madison's long straight hair settled neatly over her backless shirt, offering at least some cover. Her ripped jeans tapered off into red stilettos. It was the clothes of a stripper, not usually seen at lunch rush hour. Madison laughed and tilted her head for the benefit of the two men across from her. Raleigh watched as Madison reached out, brushed one's wrist and batted her coated thick black mascara lashes. Raleigh would never be able to pull that off without feeling like an idiot.

The man to Madison's right tilted his square jaw slightly to the crowd, and Raleigh clutched the table to stop herself from jumping under the table.

Glenn Hastin. *Her* Glenn. The ex that just wouldn't go away. Wasn't there some kind of rule about flirting with your sister's ex-fiancé? For that matter, all of Raleigh's exes should be off-limits to her sister, especially the ones suspected of murder. Considering Glenn was the second ex of hers that was a possible murderer, Madison should avoid the whole lot.

Raleigh yanked her cell phone out of her pocket and dialed Madison. She watched Madison continue flirting instead of making any move toward her vibrating phone on the table.

"Come on, pick up," Raleigh muttered, clutching her phone. Mike glanced up from the notes he printed neatly in small letters. Meticulous handwriting.

Madison's hand reached for the phone, but she studied it in her hand a moment before she answered. "What?"

"Meet me in the restroom."

"Raleigh?" Madison turned her head. "Is that you?"

Raleigh gritted her teeth. She knew her name would have appeared on the screen. Now Glenn would know she'd called. "Meet me in the restroom. Now."

"Sure thing," Madison sing sang into the phone, smiling across the table.

Mike scanned the restaurant as Raleigh stood and ducked behind a few patrons crossing to a corner table. She escaped into the hall leading to the restroom and paced the restroom with its two stalls and pedestal lavatory.

Finally, Madison burst into the restroom smiling and her eyes lit with mischievous light that Raleigh recognized as trouble and intent.

Raleigh nearly screamed out loud, but instead she said, "What are you doing?"

"Relax," Madison laughed, holding both hands up in surrender. "I knew you'd have your granny panties in a twist."

Raleigh continued to pace to prevent herself from pouncing on her. "Why are you with him?"

"As I said, relax," Madison crossed her arms. The smile didn't leave her face. "I was meeting Vince, and Glenn tagged along with him. I'm not seeing him behind your back. Chill."

"You were flirting with him."

Madison shrugged. "He's a good looking guy."

"Good looking?" Raleigh muttered. Anger rose and burned through her. Raleigh threw her hands up. "He is a suspected murderer."

The smile twitched on Madison's lips and the laugh evaporated from her eyes. "Suspected doesn't mean guilty. He didn't kill Kayla."

"How do you know that?"

Madison focused above her head. "I just do."

"How?" Raleigh's stomach fluttered. Madison's name turned up with every person questioned. How was she to be certain that Madison wasn't involved in Kayla's death? What if Madison knew who'd killed Kayla and was protecting the real killer? The answer was becoming a resounding yes that Madison was involved some kind of way.

Madison threw her shoulders back. "It doesn't concern

you."

"Like Jeffery Zedeaux thinking I'm Mason's mother doesn't concern me?"

Raleigh felt that immature streak roaring again. She'd tried so hard in the last few weeks to, well, be mature, but Madison drove her crazy. It sounded like a legitimate defense when she stood accused of dragging Madison out of here by her hair.

"Stay out of it." Madison glared at her.

"Did you talk to him and tell him the truth?"

Raleigh could see a cold, merciless anger building behind Madison's greenish blue eyes. Madison's temper had earned its own number scale in her family. It looked about a number five or six right about now.

"Stay out of my life. It's not your business."

"Then stay away from Glenn."

Raleigh's eyes widened at her own words. She'd issued an ultimatum to the queen of revenge. Raleigh's stomach bubbled with nerves and anger.

Madison's eyes narrowed and her lips puckered together. She exhaled deeply before swinging the door open and stomping out.

At the table, Mike had their food bagged and ready to go. He knew her so well. As they ducked out, she focused on the exit instead of looking back to check if Madison had returned to flirting with Glenn.

Mike glanced back though. His eyes lingered too long toward the general area where they'd sat, which told her all she needed to know.

At the door, she noticed the Tabasco tie and dark brown hair of an undercover officer Raleigh had met on one of the dates with Max. His eyes met hers and he nodded, but then he looked back in the same direction that Mike had dwelled only moments ago.

Madison's surveillance. Fine. Maybe she needed to get herself in trouble if she didn't want big sister to look out for her.

Even as she thought it, she knew it wasn't true.

Sixteen

Raleigh scrunched up her nose and her lungs constricted. Walking into a florist shop was like breaking perfume bottles. But only if that perfume was used to cover the smell of dead body decay. Death never hid itself from her, even on Valentine's Day when that poor boy had given her flowers before a junior high dance and had expected her to wear death on her wrist.

Mandy clenched sheers in one hand and a white rose in the other. Her hair was pulled back but a small chick kept sliding over her eyes that she'd blow away with a twitch of her lips. She was pretty in that blond sort of way. Not that Raleigh had anything against blonds, but she'd noticed that they required more attention. Sort of like, look at my beautiful golden tresses.

Okay, maybe she might be the tiniest bit bitter about the attention Max had given her. A girl was entitled.

Mandy's green eye's rose to see Raleigh's approach, and her jaw tensed and she bit down on her lip. "Can I help you?"

Raleigh straightened her posture. Being professional meant the bitterness had to wait. "I needed to ask you some questions about your sister."

Her eyes narrowed and her demeanor tensed. The silence grew between them as she studied Raleigh.

Moments of uncomfortableness passed before she nodded.

"Can you tell me a little bit about who your sister was?"

Mandy shrugged as she snipped the stem of a rose before sticking it into a vase. "Not much to tell. She was a pretty naïve girl who got married at nineteen to her first real boyfriend. She managed two years before the divorce six months ago."

"Was the divorce mutual?"

Her head popped up, but then she buried it again in the roses. "I wouldn't say mutual. They didn't have children or anything, but they were both bitter."

"Was Kayla dating anyone?"

Mandy exhaled. Raleigh noticed the fingers gripping the scissors were trembling. "No one I knew about. Are you and Max dating?"

"When we find time." Raleigh winced. First name basis. He'd told Raleigh to call him Max from the beginning too. "Would your sister have gone to a place like Barbeaux Bed and Breakfast willingly?"

"Did you see that? Was she forced to go there?" Her head whipped up and her eyes darted across Raleigh's face.

Raleigh shook her head. Geez. The girl was jumpy. "I only saw what she saw, and it was sort of fuzzy as if she'd been high."

"Oh, no," she shook her head. "Princess Kayla would have never tried drugs."

That type of bitterness in her voice sounded all too familiar. Maybe a little sisterly resentment? Raleigh couldn't say she didn't understand that motive.

"What about friends? Where would she hang out with them?"

"Church?" She set the shears down. "Look, I don't know. I wouldn't say we were close this last year."

"Oh?"

"It was nothing." She choked up, a tear slid down her cheek. "She wanted to be alone and didn't want my advice."

Raleigh nodded. She debated if the tears were real or a farce. She couldn't decide.

Her shoulders rose and fell. "Will you see who did this to

her?"

It would make life easy if that's how it worked. Maybe if she advertised her services, she could let all potential murder victims know to get a good look at your killer. It would increase the odds instead of all this guesswork.

"It's never that simple. Your sister didn't look at him when I ... visited her, so I didn't see."

"Oh," she said, picking the shears back up. "I can't say it's easy to believe what you are saying, but Max trusts you so I suppose it can't be wrong."

Raleigh winced at his name. Dammit. Shouldn't a guy end things before he became that familiar with someone else? She'd had enough for the moment of that too familiar closeness between the two. "Thank you. I will be in touch if I have any more questions."

Mandy nodded once, but kept her eyes on the roses.

Raleigh emerged into the sunlight and air that didn't smell like boiled eggs and dirt. She reached in her bag and was putting on her sunglasses when she bumped into someone.

"I'm sor..." she looked up into Glenn's cold eyes and stopped.

A grin spread across his lips, but it never reached his eyes.

Raleigh stepped back, her body tensing. "Are you following me?"

"No, I..." he began. "Raleigh, I just need to talk to you. I swear I never murdered anyone."

Raleigh took another step back. She felt trapped on the open sidewalk. How could she be so stupid? With Glenn lurking about, she should be paying attention to her surroundings.

Something tiny swelled inside. This was her hometown, and Glenn didn't belong here. He didn't even look like he belonged in Barbeaux Bayou in his pressed lilac shirt and gray tie.

She faced him and pushed herself to maintain eye contact. "Your personal secretary turns up buried at your construction site. How am I supposed to believe you?"

He clenched his fist. "I'm not a murderer." He stepped back and his chest heaved upward and he relaxed his fists when he exhaled. "I didn't do anything wrong. You know me; we were together for three years."

"Nothing wrong?" Was he serious? The nervousness had evaporated, replaced by a surge of anger. "What about that affair with your secretary for the last year and a half of our relationship? Nothing wrong with that, right? You should understand why murder doesn't sound like such a stretch."

His mouth opened and his eyes widened. "How do you know about that?"

"The detectives let me know while they were questioning me about you." Raleigh bit down at the anger, spitting her words. With each breath, she urged herself to calm. She may have needed to practice more because it was working as well as her relationship with her sister. "I had to hear about your midnight trysts at the construction office from a detective who thought I'd killed your lover out of jealousy. The same lover who I'd attended parties with and had asked to serve in our wedding."

His neatly manicured hand rubbed the top of his head. "They didn't tell me they told you. They promised they'd keep it from you."

"Yes, so for you omission isn't the same as lying."

"Whoa, guys." The heavy set stranger who'd sat next to Glenn at Mirv's diner stepped between them. "Glenn, why don't you take a breather inside? Give the lady a moment."

Glenn searched Raleigh's face, and the anger kept her staring straight at him instead of looking away. He stepped back and swung the door open to Mirv's diner, which was next door to the flower shop.

"I'm Vince, Ms. Cheramie." Vince stuck out a thick hand.

Raleigh hesitated a moment, but reached out into his rough grip. Damn those Southern manners.

"Raleigh, please." She breathed in deeply and waited for that nervous trembling to set in. The anger hadn't left yet.

Vince wore a black t-shirt and husky jeans. With his dark hair, large build, and olive complexion, he could blend in well here. Stark difference from Glenn. "How do you know Glenn?"

Vince nodded his head to the right. "Until about a year ago, I worked for Glenn in Texas. But then my ex-wife needed help keeping my son in line, so I moved back here."

"Oh." Raleigh paced a bit. Boss and employee. Knowing Glenn, Vince was being used for Glenn's own convenience. Not to mention he'd get nowhere here as an outsider unless he had a tour guide.

"Not a big deal." Vince grinned. "I missed my son, and I spent all my free time here. The place is part of you, you know?"

"And you're friends with Madison, too?"

Vince shrugged. "Madison's more about getting others to do what she wants than about being a friend."

Interesting. So what exactly was Vince doing for Madison then and did it have something to do with Kayla? The ringing of her cell phone in her pocket interrupted the train collision her thoughts had decided to jump onto.

She gave Vince a small smile before picking up. Me'Maw's coarse voice carried through the line and warmed her. "Dear, I hoped you could bring me see Margaret at the hospital."

Raleigh looked down at her watch. She was supposed

to do a meeting for the story in an hour. "Wasn't Madison supposed to bring you today?"

Me'Maw humphed into the phone. "I guess she's running late, and I don't want to miss visiting hours."

Figures. What did Madison do with all the hours of time she went missing? Maybe she should ask to get in on her police surveillance. She must keep those guys jumping. "I'll be there in a few minutes."

Raleigh stuffed her phone into her pocket again and looked up at Vince who was watching her with curious toffee eyes.

"I have to go," Raleigh said. "Maybe another time you can fill me in on your theory about my sister."

He chuckled, a hearty sound coming from deep in his chest. "I try not to get involved in family wars."

His laughter ceased, and he stuck out his hand. She hesitated again but shook it. At least he hadn't tried to hug her, which is what everyone else in Barbeaux Bayou did as a greeting and a good-bye.

"It was good to meet you. I can put a face to Glenn's stories now."

Raleigh scrunched her nose. "I'm sure none of it is true."

Raleigh hurried toward the ally of the downtown area where her car was parked. Paranoid that Glenn would follow her, she looked back several times, but she was alone. The sidewalk was uneven and required a walker's full attention, so she tripped several times on her brief walk. The new bakery had potted plants out front that she had to navigate, and she glanced inside the window to see the bistro tables and filled cases of pies. Its lime green walls and black trim were cute and modern and stuck out like a sore thumb among all the old buildings. Raleigh would be sure to try it soon.

Eight minutes later she pulled up at Me'Maw's front

porch, and in her robin egg blue hat, Me'Maw hobbled to the car. They reached the hospital nine minutes after the visiting hour began. Raleigh felt out of breath from the hurry and none of it had involved working and most certainly not running.

Mrs. Margaret's room was the last door down the intensive care unit with its incessant buzzing that spilled from its oversize rooms. Near room five, an older rumpled man sat in a heavy yellow chair near her door that had to have been snatched from the waiting room. The chair's occupant held his head in his enormous hands. Tiredness etched creases and dark lines across his face.

He looked toward them and half his lips curled into a smile that ended up more like a grimace, but he remained silent, his heavy eyelids speaking his pain for him. On the other side of the heavy door, Me'Maw muttered "her son" and continued her shuffle toward the hospital bed behind a half-drawn curtain.

Jitters raced through her as Ms. Margaret's still figure came into view. Machines beeped near the head of the bed, but her feathered face framed by white sheets offered no sign of life.

Raleigh strained forward, waiting for a voice or a feeling in the shadows of that open space in her brain. If she rested somewhere between life and death, shouldn't that place fall in Raleigh's open space? No stirrings in the dark recesses though. She looked away from Ms. Margaret's frozen face. Coward, she muttered to herself.

She saw death, but the in between was kind of creepy.

The bare white walls made it obvious that there was only emptiness in this room. The cards had said death would come.

Raleigh shuddered. "Me'Maw, I'm just going to wait outside."

Me'Maw nodded, and Raleigh escaped. She breathed in deeply the smell of antiseptic and urine. Maybe she should begin practicing shallow breathing. A side effect of connecting to death was an increase sensitivity to smell.

The son still sat in the same position as they'd left him. From his forehead creases and sagging neckline, she thought he might be about thirty years older than her, at least. They'd grown up on the same street, yet Raleigh had never met him. That just didn't happen in Barbeaux Bayou. Ms. Margaret had been a widow for twenty-nine years, but where had the son gone?

"I know who you are." His high-pitched voice startled Raleigh out of her thoughts.

She smiled. Her polite southern manners weren't certain what was called for in this situation.

His heavy chest heaved forward in a deep exhale. "It would have been easier if you would have let her die. I wouldn't have to decide."

Her body warmed as she gaped at him. How did one answer that? She was certain that books on manners didn't address this little scenario. Her only thoughts weren't fit to be spoken or written down.

The silence grew as her brain searched for an answer.

"I'm sorry," Raleigh said. The catchall that covered everything these days. She wasn't sorry though. It's not like she invited people to connect to her.

"I don't choose to connect to people."

He looked up at her startled. Her thoughts circled. For once, couldn't it all come out of her mouth the right way? She inhaled through her lips.

"People seek me out. I don't choose to see death. They come to me because they want to be found."

He opened his mouth to speak, but she continued. "Your mother didn't want to die alone. My helping her to do that was what she wanted. I help the dying not the living."

That strange surge through her must be pride. She didn't feel that very often.

Me'Maw emerged through the door and patted him on the shoulder. "Francis, let us know if we can help you in anyway."

Francis nodded. His eyes clouded and the years melted away until he was a ten-year-old boy staring helpless at his mother's friend.

The living were much more complicated than the dead. Maybe traiteur to the dead wasn't so bad after all.

Seventeen

Raleigh woke with a start, and her brain told her she'd slept too long. She glanced over to the brown nightstand covered in a white lace dolly where the alarm clock confirmed her suspicion. She bounced out of bed, tripping over her own coverings and scrambled for clothes, grabbing what lay on top of the nearest box.

She pulled and tamed her hair into a ponytail, cursing her memory. Why couldn't she remember to turn on the damn alarm clock? After three times in one month, most would have learned to flip the thing on by now.

She had yanked on one boot before Me'Maw called her from the kitchen. She grabbed the other boot and hobbled down the hall, hoping Me'Maw hadn't cooked some sit down breakfast this morning. She barely had time to grab a Twix before she was officially very late for work.

Paw was making a dent in his scrambled eggs and bacon and Me'Maw sipped from her cream coffee cup. Me'Maw wore her pink check duster and Paw hadn't put his shirt on over his undershirt yet. This was the usual morning routine at the house, including her rushing for work. Me'Maw pointed to the kitchen table when Raleigh emerged from the hallway.

"Flowers just came for you."

If Flo's Flowers had delivered, then she was later than usual. She yanked the card from its plastic prongs and in neat print the card read, "I'd like a chance."

The card was unsigned.

She crumpled it up and tossed it in the nearby trash bin. Glenn had sent her flowers after an argument. Now that she thought back on it, the florist had a good thing going in that situation. She once thought it cute, but now the flowers made her stomach turn. Decay lingered between the heavy perfume of the pink tips. Glenn had remembered they were her favorite of roses.

But since she'd let death back in and opened the connection, flowers attached to their roots would be her only favorite.

She grabbed the vase and headed toward the screen door to toss them in the outside bin. Madison pranced through the door with an armful of clothes and Raleigh stopped mid step. She scanned the thick pile of textured skirts, and stripped pants, and cotton and satin shirts. Price tags dangled from the items loaded down in her arms.

"Ree," Madison said, staring at the items in her arms as if she had to discover with her bare eyes a wrong stitch. "I wanted your advice on an outfit for an interview."

"Where did it all come from?"

Madison bit down on her lip. "I really want this job so I want to be sure I'm dressed modest."

So many price tags. Raleigh tried to add up the dangling numbers, but it was too much for her head to handle. "Did you buy all of these clothes?"

Madison looked up at her and squinted her eyes in a cross way. "Well, I didn't steal them if that's what you're implying."

"No, that's not what I'm implying. Where did you get the money for all of this?"

"I have a job." She clutched the pile of clothes tighter to her chest.

"Forgive me for not knowing that considering your parents and grandparents are forced to pay all of your bills because you don't have any money."

"Stay out of my business, Raleigh- I've-never-had-a-hard-time Cheramie."

Paw's chair scraped the floor and he hobbled out the house. Raleigh flinched as the screen door snapped too loudly behind him.

Madison smirked. "See what you've done."

"You are taking advantage of this family."

"And you aren't? Don't you live here too?"

Raleigh drew her shoulders up. Arguing with Madison wasn't going to help. She needed to get everyone else to stop giving into her. "Return the clothes and pay your own bills. That's my advice to you."

Raleigh set the flowers down on the kitchen counter and stomped out onto the back porch, allowing the screen door to snap shut behind her.

On the porch, she inhaled a shaky breath and then trapezed toward the garden, which began about fifty yards from the back porch and stretched out for half a mile. She headed toward the distant figure of Paw who'd walked far to burn off his anger.

She was out of breath when she caught up to him with a stitch in her side. She may need to get more exercise if she felt this out of shape from a quick jog.

"I'm sorry, Paw." Raleigh wheezed out, falling into step beside him. "I didn't mean to lose my temper."

Paw bobbed his head down twice. " 's alright. Someone needs to tell her she's wrong, and I guess none of us have the heart to. You've managed to turn out alright Raleigh Lynn."

He didn't look at her, but a grin did appear on his lips.

All the tension left her. Paw's seal of approval. She'd forgotten what that felt like. As a girl, she'd skip behind him through these rows, hoping he'd noticed her with his sparse compliments. She'd been his favorite then; everyone had known it.

"Families always have problems." Paw pulled a shelled peanut from his pocket. "Maybe you should start with that young lady's family."

Raleigh nodded. "Maybe she had a problem in the family?"

Paw shrugged. "We always know when something bad is going on; we just don't always ask the right questions. Sometimes we just don't want to confirm our suspicions."

She wasn't sure if he was talking about Kayla or Madison. It sounded like both. With each turn, Madison was implicated further, and Raleigh's family didn't know this.

Keeping it secret in a town that gossiped about everything from lovers to the groceries in one's basket would be troublesome. Ruling out Madison as a suspect may become top priority if she didn't want her family to be the topic of more gossip.

Thirty-seven minutes late for work, she pulled out of the driveway only to have Uncle Camille flag her down from his front yard. She pulled to the side of the narrow street, her car half in the overgrown grass of his yard. Someone needed to do something. Joey had come to cut the grass, and Uncle Camille had chased him away with a string of curses not fit for ears.

She opened the car door and braced herself for whatever foul temper he had for her today.

"Girl, get over here and help me inside."

Raleigh cringed, but as the good family girl she was— okay so that may be stretching it—she headed toward his plastic lawn chair under his oak tree.

She scrunched up her nose as she lifted his bone thin arm from the chair. He smelled like urine and tobacco mixed with dampness, and when he leaned on her, he was as light as a rag doll.

He hobbled to the front cement steps, straining with pain for each step. "I hear you getting into more trouble."

"Not at all Uncle Camille." Raleigh gritted her teeth. A favor to her father was to kill Uncle Camille with kindness. It might kill her as she wrangled with self-control. "Just helping people like we do."

"Helping the dead ain't helping people." he spit into the grass. "You never going to help people."

"I do, and I will after you train me."

He shook his head. "I'm going to train someone else. Jolie is a real nice girl, don't you think? She says she wouldn't mind learning."

Raleigh bit down on her lips, forcing herself not to recoil from him. "If Me'Maw thinks it's okay, then you do what you like."

He laughed, but it caused a coughing fit to come over him. His body rattled, and tipped too far to the right. His leg had given out on him. She didn't have to look at him to feel the cancer in his bones. The stench of death lay right on the surface. Her chest constricted in grief. Not all for the ornery old man, but more for the fact that she'd feel the death of her loved ones.

"I don't need mom's permission," he said, clearing his throat. "It's my choice. My choice alone."

Raleigh released him on the porch, relieved to let his arm go. Standing near him was too close to death.

She stepped back and looked at his hunched over navy Dickies, and under the morning sun and crisp cool air, the clarity of disappointment welled in her chest. How much she'd wanted it crystallized. She'd needed to be able to connect to the living, so that she didn't feel death all the time. She needed to feel life to offset the loneliness of loss. He'd taken that hope away from her.

"Why?" The word tumbled out before she could catch it.

His yellowish tinged eyes glared down at her. "You let my baby die. It was you."

No matter what else, connecting to the dead meant

dealing with the grief of the living. Raleigh shook her head and walked back to the car.

She could have argued that Madison hadn't saved his daughter, but it didn't matter. None of it mattered during grief.

She deserved a Twix. The limitations on her candy addiction couldn't apply in these situations. She couldn't go back home or she'd have to explain it to Me'Maw, so she pulled into the empty parking area of the convenience store near the bridge. Its hunter green roof and tan brick exterior dated it to her lifetime, unlike most of the buildings in Barbeaux. The gas station that was once in the same spot had been destroyed by Hurricane Andrew, and had been built as a replica but with modern materials.

Lucy Sonet was leaning over the counter smacking on pink chewing gum. With her hair pulled back in a messy twist and no makeup, she looked far from the cheerleader she'd been their senior year.

At one time, that would have given her deep satisfaction, but today satisfaction came in a shiny wrapper.

"If it isn't Ms. Raleigh Cheramie." Lucy smacked her gum.

Raleigh placed her three Twix bars down on the counter. She needed back up, of course.

"Fancy seeing you here," she said, ringing the candy up. "I'd heard you'd moved back home, but you know it's hard to believe with all the rumors that go around this town."

Raleigh smiled. It was the polite thing to do. "I came back about two months ago."

"I'm sure your family's real glad to have you back," she said, stuffing the candy into a brown paper bag. "I heard you've taken Mason back."

"What?" Raleigh asked. Her alert signals blinking.

"Yes," she said, handing over the bag. "JoAnna told me

that you came home to be his mom again. I'm sure he's thrilled."

Raleigh took the bag and stared at her. For a few moments, her words didn't register. But then they did all at once.

Jeffrey Zedeaux. Madison.

Anger flushed through her. How could a rumor like that even gain credit? Madison had walked around this town pregnant, and though she'd looked like a stick that had swallowed a peanut, she was the one who'd been pregnant.

Raleigh walked out without a word to Lucy. She had plenty words for Madison.

Eighteen

She walked into the newsroom fifty-one minutes late. If that was a sign of the day to come, this day was going to get much worse. David and Mike were bouncing around from one workstation to the other, and the room had the electricity of approaching deadline. Raleigh loved to walk into that energy, and it nearly made her forget that she wanted to kill Madison.

Barbeaux's three-day-a-week newspaper didn't produce much excitement, but they were two employees down. Phil, the advertising guy, had given his final notice two weeks ago and hadn't shown up since, and Becky, who was the layout person had gone on maternity leave eight weeks ago and hadn't given any indication of returning.

"Troubles this morning?" David glanced up at her from his computer screen.

Raleigh rolled her eyes as she slid into her station. "My family is one big trouble."

Mike's hand gripped her shoulder as he passed on the way to his station from David's office. "Who'd have thought you would be the normal one in the group?"

He grinned down at her, and she laughed. Why had she become conscious lately of how much he touched her? He'd always been like that. He had to have been. She was being ridiculous.

Four hours later, every glitch in the issue had been solved. They'd figured out the advertisements and sorted the layout, although they'd had more trial and error than success. Raleigh leaned back in her chair tingling with accomplishment.

Mike stretched his arms up to the ceiling. "Now we can get back to our research."

"That reminds me." David pulled two white tickets out of

his shirt pocket. "I'm now attending the wild game dinner as a guest of the sheriff. You two get to cover the event for Saturday's edition now."

Raleigh groaned. She hated covering fundraiser events, and she damn sure wasn't eating anything resembling a nutria or whatever else ran wild in the swamps of Barbeaux.

Mike nodded, accepting the tickets. "One story or a spread?"

"Plan for a spread." David rubbed his head. "My wife wasn't thrilled about the change of plans. Which, of course, is another side effect of your involvement. The other being all the questions I had to answer about the two of you to that Detective Blanch. Not a nice guy." He looked down, his glasses sliding further down the bridge of his nose.

She wasn't thrilled with her involvement either. And, it looked like Blanch had begun his rounds delving into their lives to prove his case. If the questions were about both of them, she knew what direction this case was going. She'd guess she was now suspected of being his accomplice.

Mike looked over at her. "What do you say date? I promise I'll pick you up on time."

He grinned to lessen the sting, but it didn't help much. She couldn't be mad at Mike though; they'd shared dirt pies together.

Mrs. Betty Marjorie, the building's main secretary who should have retired twenty years ago, opened the main door to the office with a bouquet of pink roses.

Raleigh's insides clenched. He wouldn't send flowers twice in the same day. Overboard wasn't going to help matters. He had to know this.

"Ms. Cheramie, these beautiful flowers have arrived for you." Ms. Marjorie hobbled toward Raleigh's cubicle. "Someone must think you're special."

Raleigh accepted the glass vase, her nose scrunching

up as a whiff filled her with their strong aroma. She pulled the card from the plastic picks after placing the vase on the nearby desk.

"I'm so sorry. Let me make it all up to you. Please."

Raleigh crumpled the notecard up and tossed it into the basket near her desk. "Ms. Betty, why don't you put them up front to spruce up the lobby?"

"What a lovely idea." Ms. Betty never made eye contact with anyone as she retrieved the vase and puttered back through the office door.

David muttered as he walked back to his office. "Flowers. Maybe she'd like flowers."

Mike grabbed his jacket as she grabbed her purse. "Do you have something against flowers or the person who sent them?"

"Both actually," Raleigh said, following him out. "Since the dead found that empty space in my head, flowers smell like death."

Mike stared down at her, a grin spreading across his charmingly good-looking, sun-kissed face. She knew many women who made fools of themselves over him. Why was he single again?

Raleigh frowned. "The flowers come unsigned, but I'm certain they are from Glenn."

"Both then." Mike nodded. "I suppose a guy really shouldn't send you flowers for Valentine's Day."

Raleigh climbed into his Jeep. "I'd love a guy forever if he sent me one of those candy baskets. Chocolate is the way to my heart."

Mike chuckled. "Good to know if I ever mess up."

She couldn't help but notice how easy it was with him. No stress. No worries about where she stood in his life. He'd never stand her up. Why couldn't it be that easy with Max? Maybe she was spoiled with relationships that came naturally because of the years she'd been friends with a man. She'd known Mike her entire life and Max only for two months.

She needed to stop thinking about Max. She didn't want to be one of those women who obsessed about the man who didn't pay attention to her.

"What if I was wrong about Glenn?"

Talk about a change of topic. It was her specialty these days.

"You weren't wrong." Mike looked over with is eyebrows furrowed as he pulled onto the highway. "Even if he didn't kill the woman, he cheated on you. Don't feel guilty about leaving him."

"I know." Raleigh looked out the window. "But accusing someone of murder is different than breaking up with them because they are a pig."

Mike shook his head. "You have good instincts about people. Trust them."

But that was it, wasn't it? She'd never had some instinct tell her that he was a murderer. A total jerk sometimes, yes, but nothing to tell her that she had to fear for her life.

They reached Danny's Po-Boy's two minutes late, but after a quick scan of the Po-Boy shop, Sheri hadn't turned up on time either. They selected one of the few tables empty in the corner and waited for her.

Raleigh scanned the faces of the diners until her eyes fell upon Jenny's pregnant belly. Jenny's attempts at blackmailing Madison had failed, but she'd proven herself crazy. She was also pregnant with Kyle Allemand's baby, and the rumors had him back with his wife now. Raleigh was glad they had not sat in Jenny's table section. That was one awkward conversation she didn't want to have at lunch.

Sheri sauntered into the restaurant and more than a few heads turned as she sank into her chair. It could have been the turquoise streak of hair appearing like a peacock or maybe it was the Kelly green top she wore belted over leggings that drew an audience. Sheri was her own fashion rule.

But she did resemble a peacock today.

"Sorry, I'm late." she apologized breathlessly. "I had a color that ran over."

Their waitress, Holly, took their order for the roast beef po-boys, which were the best item on the menu, and then they delved into the real reason they were having lunch since Sheri only had a short time.

"I was able to find out from Ms. Arlene that her ex-husband Skip is a charter fisherman. He has a boat down at Arpent boat sheds."

Mike leaned back in his chair. "So he will be hit or miss if we drop in."

Sheri nodded. "Arlene said he pretty much lives on that boat working on it and cleaning it. Charter fishermen usually go out real early and come in early in the afternoon."

"We might get lucky." Raleigh stuffed a fry in her mouth. If unhealthy food didn't taste so good, she wouldn't have to worry about her thighs. Someone should start working on making broccoli taste like chocolate.

Mike raised his eyebrows. She understood him to mean that luck was his territory. Her strategy usually involved perseverance. She could annoy someone well until they relented.

They were finishing their lunch when Raleigh looked up to see Vince sliding into the empty chair next to Sheri.

"Hello, Raleigh. Just thought I'd drop in and say hello." He smiled at her with lingering eye contact, but then he looked up to Mike and then to Sheri. "I'm Vince... I'm sure I've seen ya'll around."

Sheri's lips smacked together in her inquisitive pucker. An

uncomfortable silence fell over the table. Had Glenn sent him to talk to her?

Mike's arm dangling over the back of her chair stiffened. "I remember you from a construction site or two. How do you know Raleigh?"

"Oh, we have a mutual friend." Vince's gaze burned into her, and her skin warmed. Glenn wasn't her friend, and he was making her uncomfortable even implying it.

Mike frowned as he looked at her. She didn't need to read minds to know what he was thinking. They knew every person in each other's lives.

"We were just leaving for an interview." Raleigh stood. "I don't know if Glenn put you up to this, but you can tell him that sending you to talk to me isn't going to work."

She headed for the door, knowing that Mike would follow behind her after only a few heartbeats. Why wouldn't Glenn go away? Didn't he have a job? In Texas? She inhaled outside and filled her lungs to slow her pulse. The door swung open and Vince emerged with Mike close on the heels of his rugged boots.

"I'm sorry," Vince said, stopping close to her. "I just wanted to say a friendly hello. I will admit that he wanted me to talk to you for him, but I get that you don't want that. I promise not to try anymore. From now on, it will just be a friendly hello."

Raleigh studied his soft brown eyes and sad tilt of his head. His expression appeared earnest. Maybe he was telling her the truth, but she couldn't tell anymore. She had questioned her instincts since she hadn't believed Glenn capable of murder.

"Okay." Raleigh released a deep breath slowly. A hello had never killed anybody. It wasn't as if she'd run into him often. "As long as it's not about Glenn. That's done."

Mike stepped closer to her in a protective gesture. His

stony face stared down on Vince, but he didn't say anything. Though Mike rose a good three inches above Vince, Vince's husky frame made him twice Mike's size. Raleigh did not need any male macho contests.

"Good," Vince grinned. "So we're cool then?"

"Yes." Raleigh's lips rose half-heartedly into a smile. "We really need to get to that interview now."

Vince nodded. "See you around."

Mike steered her toward the parked Jeep without a word, and they headed further down Barbeaux Bayou on the back road towards Bois and Arpent boat shed.

"I hate to say this," Mike said after a few minutes of deep thought. "Maybe you need to ask Max to scare Glenn off. Maybe coming from the local police, it might convince him to leave."

Mike's tone sounded like he'd prefer she never ask Max for anything...ever. Did he hate Max? Max had stood her up, and he hadn't liked that, but the guy had been pretty decent to him until this latest debacle. Was it some kind of male dominance issue? Mike had never been possessive over their friendship. There'd been those few moments that she'd questioned, but that was just her imagination.

"That might complicate the situation even more."

Mike's focus remained on the road. Things were too serious inside this vehicle.

"Is this why you don't date a woman more than a date or two?"

After it was out, she thought maybe that hadn't been the right direction to go in to lighten things up.

Mike's gaze darted towards her and then returned to the road. "I just haven't met anyone I've wanted to see more than that." He grinned. "I guess you can say I'm holding out for the right one."

Raleigh giggled. "Funny, I never pegged you as the

romantic."

"That's because you've never let me take you out on a date."

Raleigh laughed with him, but her thoughts slammed into overdrive. Did that mean he had wanted to take her out? It couldn't be. Her brain was overthinking it. She needed to stop because she wasn't going to mess this friendship up. She needed him in her life. She would not make things weird.

At Arpent boat shed, they asked a guy carrying an ice chest where Skip Guidry's boat was docked, and they walked along the wharf toward Slip Seventeen. She was aware of the dirty water lapping against the dock. She still felt queasy when she was near, but as long as she wasn't in the water, she'd discovered her legs didn't turn to jelly fish tentacles and her throat didn't close up. Each day back in Barbeaux quelled a little of her phobia. Maybe if she lived to a hundred, she'd get over it.

Raleigh recognized his blond haired beach look on sight. She'd never met him personally but she had watched Madison take an envelope from him the day of the boucherie.

What the hell would Madison be doing with Skip Guidry, ex-husband of the murder victim?

Mike handled the introductions and Raleigh used the time to study him. He was shirtless and his chest was impeccable. He only had on board shorts and deck shoes, topped by his shaggy blond hair. It was December and even though the temperature had reached the eighties today, usually you didn't see shirtless at this time of the year, even in Louisiana.

His tan was the color of baked toffee. The shirtless peck show must be how he kept it all year long. He also spent many hours in the gym from the looks of it, which made the shirtless view so much nicer.

"We just had a few questions about your wife," Raleigh inserted, drawing his attention toward her.

He grinned, his hazel eyes flashing. "A fine piece of work."

Raleigh tilted her head, studying him. "How so?"

"Wouldn't have sex until we were married, but after our divorce chased every man with a pulse and landed quite a few as I've heard."

Raleigh gulped. It always caught her by surprise how easily people around here divulged personal information. Getting information didn't require prying skills.

"Who ended the marriage then?"

His lips straightened into a thin line. "She wanted the divorce."

"Why?" Raleigh again tilted her head and held his eye contact.

"I had an affair," he said nonchalantly, unblinking. It rolled off his tongue so easy as if he'd said he liked hot sauce on his fries.

Raleigh nodded. "Her sister said it was a messy divorce."

"She should know," he sputtered out. He blinked and the crinkles in the corners of his eyes deepened. "She seduced me. Don't believe anything that leech has to say. All she wanted was to ruin her sister's perfect life as she once said. You know that bitch had the nerve to video tape us and then send it to her sister in an email?"

He shook his head but the grin didn't leave his lips. He was actually proud of this. Most people would have only confessed to this in a life or death situation. At least she would hope. She didn't like this guy.

So obviously the sister's grief had been an act if Skip was telling the truth. Was the act all for Max's sake or to cover the murder? Max had bought into the act completely.

Shouldn't he have caught on by now if he was investigating? Her stomach clenched.

Mike cleared his throat. "Did you still speak to your ex?"

"Nah," he said, shaking his head. "I got the boat. She got the house. I heard she wasn't speaking to any of her family. Something about her parents disapproving of the divorce. I think it had more to do with her giving her sister a black eye at her family reunion though."

Okay, so she'd thought her family was a little crazy. They didn't compare to this circus.

Mike thanked him for his time, and they returned to the Jeep.

"I think we need to talk to the sister again."

Mike nodded. "Something tells me that she should be our number one suspect at the moment."

Raleigh agreed, although she had also involuntarily added Madison as a suspect in her mental list. She wasn't ready to admit to anyone, including her oldest friend, where her suspicions were taking her. Maybe Max should hear all of this so he could stop comforting Mandy. That would sure offer Raleigh comfort.

Nineteen

Raleigh knocked over the box by the door in her haste to find her clothes, and then stubbed her toe on the box next to it as she picked it up. She swore as pain shot up her leg. It was time she did something about these boxes. No one should live out of cardboard boxes unless they were homeless.

And she wasn't homeless, even if her sister didn't believe that she should live at her grandparents. Me'Maw would never put her out. Even though the adult thing would be to get her own place, she'd miss Me'Maw's cooking and company. As she saw it right now, moving out offered only one perk and that was distance between her and Madison.

She scanned the scattered mess again. Mike would be here any moment and she couldn't find her other heel.

"Raleigh Lynn," Paw called from the hall.

Her heart increased its pace as it had when she was a girl and he'd called her to him. Paw reserved first and middle name for big trouble, though he'd slipped the other day with a compliment. She didn't know of anything she'd done today to warrant her "you're in hot water" name, but compliments didn't come that close together either.

She spied the shoe under a pile of clothes and hobbled out into the hall. He waited for her about halfway down where an old canvas painting of a duck hung on the wall. Cousin Joey had painted it long ago as a teenager.

"We need you in the kitchen."

Paw was a man of few words, but he left no room for puzzling over his meaning. She slipped her shoe on as she hopped on one foot toward the kitchen. At the table, Madison was staring off into space with a scowl on her face. Their dad leaned against the back door frame still in his dirty work clothes with his arms crossed across his chest.

Me'Maw leaned forward in her usual rocker. Paw had gathered all the major decision makers. Uh, oh. She began to think that trouble was brewing especially from the grim expressions all around. "What's wrong?"

Me'Maw smiled, a half-hearted attempt at best that didn't reach her cheeks. "Nothing's wrong. There's just something to discuss."

Paw eased himself into his usual chair, bones cracking as he did. "We are offering you Aunt Clarice's old house."

Her dad's boots stomped down as he stepped closer. "If you don't want it, and it's okay if you don't, the house will be placed for sale."

Madison's fist slammed down on the table. "You can't do that. *I've* paid on that house."

Dad's hand rose in a stop motion and his lips were set sternly. Raleigh waited for the train wreck she foresaw coming. "Alex paid for that house. You paid two months of your own money, and your grandparents have had to cover for you more months than that. I'm disappointed that you asked them in the first place, and that will no longer happen."

She had a feeling there were many discussions before this meeting was called with the two of them there.

Madison's green eyes burned into Raleigh. "I hate you. My life was pretty good until you came home. I wish you'd go back to wherever the hell you got lost at before, little Miss Perfect Princess."

Madison stood up, sending her chair rocking back on its legs. She stormed out, careful not to go near the reach of their father.

She'd called it. Train wreck. She'd have to hold off on the questions for her sister about Kayla's death or she might be her sister's next victim. She regretted the thought as soon as it popped into her head. She sure hoped her sister hadn't

163

killed Kayla. This family had enough scandals without adding to it.

Paw looked at her. "We know this might be quick for you, so we are going to give you a few days to sleep on it."

Dad's head bobbed up and down. "Your mom and I can help you with the first payment since it's due in a week, but you were right. We can't expect them to pay for a second house."

Raleigh nodded. Her eyes burned as though she needed to cry, and she wasn't sure why. Madison's words had stung, but her father's admittance felt like a small victory. All too confusing to dwell on at this moment in time.

The Jeep's horn honked from the driveway outside.

"I will let you know what I decide in the next couple of days."

Her dad nodded.

Paw rapped his knuckles on the table. "Old man Wilbert always went to that dinner. If you see him, tell him hello for me."

Raleigh smiled. "Next time I'll get you tickets so you can tell him yourself."

Paw leaned back in his chair with a grin.

Raleigh patted her dad's arm on the way out. Her mother's absence indicated disapproval, but at least most of the family had come around.

The chill of the night air left her as soon as she sank into the toasty Jeep. Mike was nodding his head and tapping his fingers on the steering wheel to the music waiting for her.

"Running late?" Mike pulled out of the driveway, sliding across the road as if they were in a remote control car.

"Family meeting," Raleigh muttered. She craned her neck to get a glimpse of Aunt Clarice's house as they flew past. She'd wanted a house just like it when she and Glenn had talked about their first home together. That was before

Muddy Grave

she'd found out that their starter home would have to make room for a mistress.

"Doesn't sound good."

Raleigh pulled her focus away from Cheramie Lane and looked at him. He smelled delicious. Earth and spice and male. He was the closest she came to a regular date these days, but she didn't get a goodnight kiss.

"They offered me Aunt Clarice's old house, and Madison told me she hated me. The usual drama."

Mike laughed with her. "Madison used to tell you that at least once a day when you two were growing up. The house isn't a bad idea though."

"You think so? Nothing says permanent like buying a house." Just two months ago she'd reminded herself on the drive back to Barbeaux Bayou that she'd never wanted to return home... ever. Things had changed quickly, and she wasn't sure she'd caught up yet.

"You aren't going anywhere and you know it. It's grown on you." He glanced over and smiled, but his eyes seemed to question. "And it would give you space from the family, but you'd still be close."

Raleigh nodded. "All true statements, but can I afford it?"

"It's cheaper than any place you'd rent, and you can get a roommate if you need to have help paying it."

"It has two bedrooms. The second one isn't that big, but it is a room."

He grinned. "Hell, I'd even be your roommate. It'd be cheaper than my rent."

She'd imagine Max wouldn't jump up and down in excitement that her roommate was a man. But, she and Mike were best friends, right? No one would think anything if her best friend was a woman.

But Mike wasn't a woman her inner voice reminded her.

He was a good-looking, charming, boyishly rugged man who also happened to be single.

Living together and working together might put a strain on that friendship though. How much time could two people spend together before they wanted to strangle each other? Not that they argued now.

Tonight was requiring too much thinking.

At the door of the civic center, a young guy dressed in a penguin suit greeted them. She'd attended a few weddings here as a teenager—Cousin Joey's being one of them. She was always surprised by how they managed to turn a wooden basketball floor into a formal venue with a few potted plants.

Another penguin ushered them to a round table toward the center of the crowd. Raleigh scanned the room, noticing the high school social class seating. Toward the front of the room, the big donors held wine glasses, toasting their accomplishments. Jeffery Zedeaux mingled among the tables in his alligator print tie. He wasn't fooling anyone. He wouldn't be caught dead in that outside of this wild game dinner. The law enforcement officers and such occupied four tables to her left.

Max was staring at her as her eyes fell on him. From the deep frown that creased the corners of his lips, she could tell he was angry with her. She wasn't aware of doing anything except waiting for him to call, so she should be the one angry.

The back tables were filling up with ordinary folks whose idea of dressing up was blue jeans and a collar shirt. She probably belonged with those guys, but their place cards on the table said press.

Raleigh accepted the glass of wine Mike handed her and searched for signs of food. She was feeling a little trepidation over the menu. Was it rude to refuse something?

Not that she hadn't had occasion to be rude before. But Mike handled food stories for a reason.

Mimi Blanch directed the serving staff near long white table clothed tables. At least with Alex's admission about Claudia's death and her own son's involvement, Ms. Blanch had returned to pretending Raleigh didn't exist. Raleigh saw no reason to change that. It's not like Raleigh's income placed her anywhere within reach of Mimi Blanch's social status, and all the local charities she worked tirelessly for were run by committee so Raleigh could interview someone else when she was assigned a story.

Mike pointed to a young flustered looking woman. "She's the one."

Raleigh gulped her wine and waited as she approached them. She didn't wait long. The woman walked at an unnatural pace.

"Good evening." She whipped out a sheet from her clipboard and handed it to Mike. "This is a pretty standard press release with all the basics spelled out for you."

Her eyes hid behind small-framed glasses and darted from Mike to her in cartoon squirrel fashion. Raleigh had to smile and force the laugh back down her throat.

A long thin, unpolished finger pointed toward the front table. "Those individuals are the organizers of the event. They have been told to expect questions at the end of the speech portion of the evening. Will you be needing anything else?"

Mike glanced down at the clipboard. "Can I call you tomorrow to get final totals of the fundraising?"

She pulled out a business card from a tiny pocket in her navy blue pantsuit and handed it over. "This is my personal number. You can use it for whatever you like."

She smiled at him, her dusty blue eyes lighting against her blond hair. She then turned on her black heel and sauntered away. This time in slow motion and a definite uplift in her backside.

Raleigh frowned. Why did that always happen? He certainly wasn't single for lack of options.

"She was flirting with you." Raleigh studied him beneath her eyelashes.

He was skimming the press release and hadn't even watched her walk away. "Not my type."

"What is your type?"

Mike shrugged. "Dark hair. My own generation. Maybe a nose for trouble, you know."

He looked up from the page finally and grinned at her.

Raleigh laughed, but her neck warmed. Had he just described her? Couldn't have. "So a pretty broad selection then."

A tapping on the microphone vibrated through the room. Mimi Blanch stood on the makeshift stage looking perfectly together in her alabaster suit. Raleigh sipped from her wine glass as Mimi joked and laughed, a red-lipped fake smile plastered across her wrinkle free complexion.

Since her forehead and eyebrows didn't budge, Raleigh suspected cosmetic help to remain that youthful-looking. Raleigh rolled her eyes, but then guiltily scanned the room. She unconsciously sought out Max. He was leaning back in his chair, glowering at an empty spot in space. She didn't know what he was upset about. He'd stood her up. Shouldn't he have asked her out by now? Maybe with groveling and gifts involved.

His eyes slid into hers and they gazed at each other a moment. Had he moved onto Mandy? Anger smoldered in his eyes, and for the life of her, she couldn't figure out why.

As Mimi Blanch allowed the dinner to commence, Raleigh excused herself to step outside into the cool air. Her lungs felt as if they couldn't fill in the stuffiness of the crowded room. The chill of the outside air prickled her feverish skin, and she inhaled from deep within her chest.

Raleigh closed her eyes and the darkness swallowed the lampposts. She stood in a doorway staring at a green door with a cheap, tarnished gold handle. She stumbled, her ankle sliding off a heel, and a strong grip yanked her back and her eyes popped open to Max's smoldering eyes glaring down on her.

"Why didn't you tell me you were going to be here tonight?"

His anger was so accusing, and she felt her defenses kick in. He'd jumped right into an argument without a mention about her slipping into a dead girl's last moments. Not that he could have known, but a hello, how are you doing would have covered it.

"Probably the same reason you didn't mention it."

His hand released its grip on her arm and looked away. "It was last minute. Chief wanted everyone involved on the case here."

She was having a difficult time focusing on Max. Had the hand been only Max's hand in her present or had someone grabbed Kayla? It probably wasn't a good thing that she couldn't distinguish the difference anymore.

"We had to cover the event because David is with your group."

"Damn, Raleigh," he spat out, his hands on hips creasing his jacket. "Are the two of you always together?"

Was that jealousy in his tone?

He waved his arm and the lamplight lit his taunt face. "Everyone thinks the two of you are a couple. Do you have any idea how people look at me when I tell them we are dating?"

Raleigh's face warmed. People talking about her. Again. Is this what they meant by small-town celebrity? Well, they could have it. "Aren't you the one who's always working and canceling dates? You have a partner too."

"It's not the same and you know it."

"Well then..." Raleigh's anger built. How had this all turned on her? "What about Mandy? She has more of your attention than I've had in weeks."

"She's work," Max shook his head, combing his fingers through his thick hair. "I have two open murder cases right now on my desk. People want answers, and she's helping with the case."

Like she had when her sister was abducted? She didn't feel assured by his answer. And two murders? Had she missed a death?

"Mike is my best friend." Raleigh tried to focus, but her thoughts raced over a murder she'd missed. Someone hadn't sent her an invitation. "He's not going away. Maybe if you'd actually show up for a date, people would know we were dating."

Max gazed off into the parking lot. His expression gave nothing away to what thoughts were working through his mind. "We'll discuss this tomorrow. I have to get back inside."

Raleigh kept her mouth closed, though it pained her to do so. All they did anymore was put things off until another time. Including an actual date.

The glass door swung closed behind him, and Raleigh relaxed. Exhaustion came over her like a summer storm. She had a story to write though, and tomorrow she planned to find out about this second murder.

She stepped toward the door just as it swung open to reveal Skip and Jeffery Zedeaux. Instinctively, she stepped back from them, but immediately regretted it. She should have walked through them, now they were facing each other.

"If it isn't Raleigh Cheramie," Jeffery smirked, the cold smoldering behind his eyes.

Skip frowned, looking from Raleigh to Jeffery.

"I was just going back inside," Raleigh said, straightening her spine and raising her chin.

"Skip," Jeffery said, turning to him. "Have you had the unfortunate opportunity to meet Raleigh Cheramie?"

Skip's frown deepened. He clearly wasn't certain what was going on here.

"We have met, Jeffery," Raleigh said. "I didn't realize he kept your company."

Jeffery laughed though the humor didn't touch his face. "Speaking of company. Skip, did you know that Raleigh has a son that she sent back here to be raised by her sister?"

His self-satisfied smirk was too much for her.

"Actually, Jeffery," Raleigh tilted her head and smiled. "I don't know who misinformed you, but obviously it wasn't one of the many residents who saw Madison walking around pregnant, looking like a twig had swallowed a pine cone. I'm only Mason's aunt."

Skip continued his look back and forth between the two, squirming in the place he stood.

Jeffery's eyes narrowed. "You're lying."

"Afraid not," Raleigh laughed. "I missed the birth entirely. See, I was living in Texas. Had just moved in fact. Madison had to stop stripping the last four months of her pregnancy. Maybe you should verify facts before you spread rumors about something you know nothing about."

He stared at her speechless. A priceless moment, one she'd probably never have again. Too bad she hadn't recorded it.

"If you excuse me, I have a story to do," Raleigh smiled. "Wouldn't want to get the facts wrong."

She walked through them and swung the door open.

She didn't know why Madison had needed him to believe that Raleigh was Mason's mother. Raleigh suspected Jeffery Zedeaux of being Mason's father, but that didn't mean Raleigh would lie for her to cover it up.

Madison had plenty to answer for these days, but Raleigh couldn't seem to work up enough nerve to ask.

Twenty

Yawning, Raleigh stumbled down the hall toward the kitchen. Between the glass of wine and the lingering anguish over Max, sleep had remained as elusive as chicken at last night's dinner. Every meat that had a reputation for tasting like chicken had been served, but she'd come home hungry. Under Mike's insistence, she had managed to do some taste testing. In hindsight, she should have tasted first and asked second.

Me'Maw rocked back and forth with her favorite mug cradled in her hands. One of her special religious motif patterned quilts covered her from her chest to the floor, and the Virgin Mary and a tattered heart stood out from the crosses and other symbols. The blues of the quilt's background brightened the velvety creases of Me'Maw's face. Sereneness had returned to Me'Maw's statue.

The floorboards had been so cold this morning that Raleigh had hopped up and down in an attempt not to touch the floor too long. Winter weather had arrived in Louisiana, but the temperature would be sure to rise again within a few days. It better. Cold weather wasn't her Christmas wish.

Raleigh pulled a Twix from the special candy drawer "Have you seen Madison this morning?"

After some thought last night, she'd decided that Madison needed to be dealt with, and by dealt with, she meant questioned and read the riot act. Hard tasks were easier when you just got them over with, and this one would be as difficult as convincing Paw and her dad to stay home on opening day of hunting season.

"Not since yesterday when she stormed out." Me'Maw raised her mug with both hands and sipped. "She'll come around. She doesn't take to change real quick."

Raleigh nodded, studying her morning chocolate. Understatement of the decade, but her plans to question her sister would have to happen anyway. "I've been thinking about Aunt Clarice's house. I do love that house, but I worry about the cost."

"It's just an offer." Me'Maw sipped her coffee. "We're not trying to stress you out, dear."

"I could take a roommate," Raleigh said, sliding into the old kitchen chair. She could feel the tiny bursts in her head as the chocolate worked through her system. She'd swear chocolate ran through her veins. "I also thought I could charge for my services. You know like the other day."

Me'Maw's lips thinned into a straight even line and her face stilled.

The chocolate wasn't firing fast enough or at least not as fast as her tongue. Me'Maw didn't like the mention of money for what they did. It was against the traditions of the traiteur. "I'll always help people who show me their death, but I could also help people who want to pay as well."

Me'Maw's face relaxed some and she rocked forward. "I suppose that would be alright. My mother took donations when times were rough."

Raleigh nodded, relieved she'd recovered that potential disappointment. She hadn't thought that through before coming out with it. Raleigh had never considered payment until she'd had it handed to her. The dead left their pocketbook behind, so seeking payment wasn't an option. But sometimes the living needed to know about the dead, and it couldn't hurt to ask for a donation. She considered this work.

On her way to work, she had a few minutes to spare so she decided to check out Aunt Clarice's house. She'd always been drawn to that house. Did she love it enough to own it, to actually commit to living in Barbeaux for a long...

long time?

It wasn't as if she planned to go anywhere else... now. She'd delayed that decision, preferring to live like a guest. A guest could decide to leave crazy behind whenever she wanted unlike the resident of the crazy house, or worse the owner of the crazy house.

The house's French door swung open as she turned the brass handle. She exhaled. She'd thought that it would be locked and Madison would have the only key.

The door creaked. In its hollowness, the house waited for some horror movie scene to unfold. Raleigh shuddered. Bare white walls and sanded pine floors stretched into doorways and hallways. Her footsteps echoed against its bareness as she walked toward the back of the house. When she reached the living room's open doorway, deep red broke the sparseness.

Madison's dark hair stuck out from the end of a stretched out sleeping bag.

Raleigh stepped into the room, and Madison bolted up.

"Damn, Raleigh," Madison spit out. "You don't know how to knock?"

"You don't live here, Madison," Raleigh answered, looking down on her furrowed brow. "No one does."

"It doesn't belong to you." Madison's lips protruded out more than necessary... pouting, not a good way to start the conversation they needed to have.

"Look," Raleigh sighed. She'd have to work up to this confrontation. "If you really want the house, you have to pay for it. No one is trying to take anything from you."

Madison sank back down in the sleeping bag. "No one wanted you here. We were perfectly happy without you."

She then pulled the blanket over her head, ending the conversation. She'd need to work or Madison's mood first. Raleigh left in frustration.

Raleigh slammed the phone down and resisted banging her head against her desk. An hour and twenty-three phone calls later, she hadn't managed to figure out the second murder victim. Did dead bodies disappear these days? From the lack of talk going on in Barbeaux today, she'd swear that rumors had disappeared along with the body.

Mike's chair creaked as he leaned back. "No luck?"

Raleigh nibbled on her bottom lip. "Max said two murders, but how come we haven't heard about a second one?"

"You could just ask him."

Raleigh rolled her eyes at him, and he chuckled.

"If you want to know, you'll have to ask."

Mike had visibly relaxed after she'd relayed her and Max's conversation of last night. His shoulders had released their tension and his ready grin had returned. He'd appreciated and puffed up a bit at her defense of their friendship. She had to wonder if he'd worried she'd drop him once she and Max were dating. They'd never done that before, even if they'd lived apart for the last seven years.

Her phone rang, and she picked it up. Ms. Betty from the front desk croaked that someone was here to see her and then hung up. Raleigh could be offended by the abruptness, but she knew it was just Ms. Betty's manner.

The front lobby was silent. The only person in the dark carpeted area was Mandy. She wore a simple flowered cotton dress that hugged her delicate frame. Mandy fidgeted with her purse strap as she stared at an oil painting of a fishing boat.

Her twitching eye turned on Raleigh and she jittered with nerves. Strange woman. And maybe crazy. "Thank goodness you are here. I haven't been able to stop thinking about my sister since we last spoke. Do you know anything else?"

Where else would she be? She did work here. Every time Mandy spoke, Raleigh couldn't help but think about how contrived her words sounded. But anyway, she and Mike were supposed to find her today to interview her again. She'd stumbled onto their doorstep instead. How convenient.

"We're investigating it."

"I just can't shake this feeling." Her voice quivered and her eyes were downcast. "I'm suffocating with all these thoughts. Has she shown you anything else?"

Raleigh imagined guilt could be suffocating. She didn't trust the tears weaving slowly down Mandy's cheeks. The woman had seduced her sister's husband. There should be feelings of self loathing involved as well.

"Nothing that leads to a murderer, I'm afraid. We interviewed Kayla's ex-husband. He had some pretty interesting revelations about your relationships."

The tears streaked down her face that became as white as the dust on the end tables in the lobby. "It wasn't like that."

"How was it, then?" Raleigh asked, noticing that Mandy hadn't asked what was said. Had Skip told her about their conversation? That would mean they'd communicated.

"Skip and I were high school sweethearts. I have loved him since tenth grade."

"Oh," Raleigh said. What kind of messed up family was this? Every time she learned something new, she had to wonder about the sanity of the people involved.

"When I went to college, we took a break. I just wanted to be sure before I married my high school sweetheart and spent my entire life with one guy. I didn't expect... well, you know."

"Did they start dating then?"

She nodded. "He was angry that I wanted a break, so when she showed interest, he decided to get back at me."

"But they got married." Even as she said it, she knew that this family didn't really hold marriage sacred.

"My sister decided she wouldn't have sex until she was married." Bitterness slipped into her voice. The tears had ceased though, and the anger beneath the weak front had shown itself. "So he married her at the courthouse within two months of their first date."

"That must have made holiday dinners uncomfortable." Raleigh sank down on her bottom lip. She needed a censor because hers wasn't quick enough these days.

Mandy laughed, the noise scratching Raleigh's ears as it echoed in the lobby. "My family thought it was wonderful that he was part of my family. They loved him."

"Still." Raleigh swallowed another remark about crazy families. Maybe the censor had arrived. "You had an affair with your sister's husband."

The anger brightened her cheeks to a pale rose pink. "I loved him." She paused, struggling for well-thought out words. Words to defend her actions. It might take awhile. "She betrayed me first. She deserved it."

And that was what you called a motive. Since she and Madison's recent bout of arguments, she could see how things could be justified in one's head. But, Kayla was dead, and someone had killed her.

"Now that they are divorced, are you two together?"

More tears spilled from her puffy eyes. "He needed a break after Kayla flipped out."

She couldn't imagine why someone would go a little crazy about her sister having an affair with her husband. Oh, wait, yes, that could drive anyone a little crazy. But it also established more of a motive. With Kayla gone, the path would be cleared for the two to be together.

Mandy had been at the bar that day too... Phil had said so. "Did you see your sister the day she went missing?"

"No." She pulled a tissue from her handbag. "We'd had an argument the week before when Skip told me he needed a break. I hadn't spoken to her since."

She hadn't blinked during the entire lie. It unnerved Raleigh. Why had that been so easy for her?

Raleigh inhaled, unable to come up with another question that didn't start with liar, liar, pants on fire. "Do you know any of her friends?"

"Just Cheyenne down at the bank, and your sister, of course." She wiped roughly at her face, red splotches emerging. "My sister went a little crazy after the divorce. In the last six months she dated about thirty men." She cleared her throat and her eyes studied something behind Raleigh. "She went home with every one of them."

Wow. That widened the suspect pool to the size of a football team. Saving yourself for marriage mustn't mean as much after a divorce. How did one go so horribly wrong though?

The entrance door swung open and a lady entered carrying an arrangement of various candy bars. Dread and anticipation swirled through her. Had Glenn moved away from flowers? How would he know that they gave her feelings of death?

The short woman with sleek cropped blonde hair smiled. "I have a delivery for Raleigh Cheramie."

Her stomach churned as she accepted the arrangement. Mandy slipped out while she signed the clipboard, but Raleigh focused on that white card sticking out of the carefully arranged dozen candy bars instead.

The card simply said, "You're beautiful."

Raleigh balled it up and tossed it into the trash. Her hand grasped the basket and dangled it for a moment over the can, but then she pulled it away. Who was she kidding? Chocolate was chocolate. Even if it came from a possible murderer.

Twenty-One

She left work frazzled. She'd spent most of the day making and receiving phone calls, and the only tidbit of relevant information she'd learned was that she wasn't cut out for telemarketing. She'd heard all about Glenda Ayo being caught with her husband's brother, and how Arthur Santia had been busted for growing pot in his mother's azaleas, but no murder rumors had trickled through the gossip lines. She'd have to ask Max who the second victim was, and that didn't cause waves of joy.

As she crept across the drawbridge in traffic, a conscious awareness of the dirty bayou water below brought a flutter in her middle. Bridges were an issue for her. Images of them falling out from beneath her ran rampant. She'd come far in the last two months, but it might be seven years before she didn't feel as if the muddy water was crawling over her skin, suffocating her.

In her determination not to notice the water below, she spotted Madison's parrot blue car parked at Sheri's shop. Something was definitely going on with Madison, and those questions about Kayla weren't going away on their own. Add Aunt Clarice's house to the equation, and sibling rivalry had reached an all time high. Raleigh didn't want to end up like Kayla and Mandy, but her suspicions weren't clearing up, only becoming more of a dilemma.

The bell jangled above Sheri's door, alerting Madison to her presence. The smile that toyed at Madison's lips disappeared, and she grimaced at her reflection in the mirror as Sheri pinned up her wet hair.

"We need to talk," Raleigh said, checking to make sure no one else was in the small shop. This wasn't a conversation to be overheard. Not if she wanted to keep them all from being hauled in again to be questioned by Barbeaux's finest.

Madison glowered at her reflection and remained silent.

"I need to know what you know about Kayla's death."

Sheri and Madison both looked her way. From Madison's raised eyebrows, she hadn't expected that question.

Madison pursed her lips. "I didn't know Kayla."

Raleigh approached the chair. "We both know that isn't true. Everyone I ask has brought you up. I'm surprised you haven't been questioned by the police yet."

"What are you accusing me of exactly?" Madison narrowed her eyes. For her part, Sheri didn't skip a beat with the snipping of Madison's ends though by the deep furrow of her eyebrows, it was taxing her concentration efforts to do so.

"I'm not accusing you of anything," Raleigh said, and then thought she probably should have considered her strategy beforehand. "You were one of the last people to see Kayla alive, and the two of you were in on some kind of business venture. So what was going on?"

Madison stared at her reflection in the mirror, her eyes unblinking. Raleigh began to think Madison was going to ignore her when her expression changed.

"Kayla and I were business partners, and I left her at Phil's with a pulse."

Well that only confirmed what she already knew. Not a productive conversation.

"What kind of business?"

"One that is none of your business," Madison snapped.

Raleigh exhaled loudly. Impossible.

"Could this business have led to her death?"

Madison's eyebrows sank further down. "No, we'd only just begun working on it."

"Did she have plans with anyone that night?"

"How am I supposed to know? Not everyone keeps tabs

on everyone like you do."

She was getting nowhere. Sadly, she'd expected this conversation to go much worse.

"Who was with her when you left Phil's?"

Madison shrugged. "She was alone. Are we done now?"

"I told Jeffery Zedeaux that I wasn't Mason's mother and that you were," Raleigh blurted. She wasn't sure why, but the need to score some kind of point in this conversation had overcome her.

Madison eyes darkened and her lips straightened. "Sheri, it would seem that my sister is back to ruining people's lives. Hope I get to watch when the next person chases her away from this town. I hope they do it with pitch forks this time."

Raleigh frowned. She supposed she asked for that one. Sheri met Raleigh's eyes, and though a frown twisted at the corners of her lips, her eyes lit with laughter.

"Sheri," Raleigh said, avoiding her sister's glare. "I'll let you know when to pencil in a housewarming party for my new home."

Madison's head swung around toward her and her eyebrows furrowed together. Raleigh saw the cold anger in her eyes. Sisterly love wasn't anywhere in that stare.

Raleigh turned and left, the bell jangling behind her. Arguing with Madison was exhausting.

Ten minutes later, Max waited with hands in front pockets leaning against Me'Maw's front porch. She stopped the car in her usual front yard parking spot and stared at him a moment.

What was the appeal? Yes, he was good-looking with his toned body, clean-cut face, and wild grey eyes. But why was she drawn to him? Was it because she couldn't have him? Hmmm. A therapy session in the car probably wasn't a good idea with the object of her dilemma standing and waiting for her near Me'Maw's Camellia bush.

She could walk past him and forget about it all. Close the door on the relationship possibility and give up. But then she'd only think about it. Best to get it over with, like yanking duck tape from flesh- hard and all at once. She imagined normal people who hadn't been tied up before didn't have that reference to make.

She stopped right in front of him and her nostrils filled with sea and spice. His shirt tugged at his shoulders and his biceps peeked out, flesh of island tan. She flushed as his magnetic presence surrounded her. Damn attraction. It was almost as bad as her temper.

"I came to apologize." He smiled and motioned to a plastic bag of Chinese food containers. They'd gone to the local Chinese restaurant on their first date where they'd sampled a little of everything. The bag overflowed with containers. As if he was trying to create that night of laughter and easy conversation.

Raleigh's insides quivered. She needed to move. "Walk with me. Bring the food."

With food in hand, he followed her without a word. She felt jittery. She'd wanted this, but it didn't feel right. Half way up the street, he grabbed her clammy hand. "I'm sorry I behaved so badly." He squeezed her hand. "I suppose jealousy isn't my strongest selling point."

" I wasn't sure you were interested in dating anymore." His hand felt warm and strong as it swallowed her own. He squeezed again.

"It's the stress of the job." In the evening sunset, his eyes flashed reflective grey and drew her in. "Cases have been all mixed up, but I shouldn't be taking it out on you."

Raleigh led him through the gate and up the porch steps of Aunt Clarice's old house debating internally about which way to go: relationship or murder investigation. Five minutes ago she hadn't believed there was a relationship, but she'd spent her entire day searching for a second victim. The urge to interrogate him was winding through her. The good girlfriend would probably know how to prioritize the two.

"I'm sorry I keep landing in the middle of your cases." Raleigh yearned to ask him about the second murder. The temptation of curiosity was tipping the scales in its favor. It was probably one of those things that would make her fail as a girlfriend.

He shook his head. "I know you don't do it on purpose. You do what you do to help people, not get in my way. It's not your fault that my bosses don't trust you."

Raleigh turned the old crystal knob on the front door, and it swung open. She'd been worried that Madison had locked the door behind her when she'd left this morning. Raleigh needed to find a key soon before she did get locked out.

They entered the front sitting area, where the sleeping bag was splayed out across the floor, and the old black leather couch was pushed up against the wall.

"It's not every case though." Raleigh stopped walking and looked at him to gauge his reaction. "I'm only involved in one of your murder cases."

A frown twitched at the corner of his lips, but his mesmerizing eyes remained on her. "It was both. Summer's autopsy came back inconclusive, so her death was ruled undetermined. I'm looking into it."

"Wait, I thought she died of a drug overdose?"

"We thought so too." Max's focus moved from her to make a sweep of the sparse room that had once been crowded with all of Aunt Clarice's mementos. It was empty now except for the black leather sofa that Raleigh needed to haul outside, cover it with gasoline, and then torch the albatross. The sofa had earned fame during Madison's budding Madame business, and Raleigh would be sure to wear gloves before she touched it due to its reputation.

Max pulled her closer. "Physical signs at the scene pointed to that." She breathed in deep the smell of him. It filled her and her flesh tingled. "No drugs in the toxicology report though."

"Wow." Raleigh's brain raced over the new information. She'd connected to Summer as she'd died. In Summer's body she'd been nauseous, and the room had spun in and out of focus, tipping over several times. Shadows had grown into giant creatures. How had there been no drugs?

She squeezed his hand. "Could it be a mistake? When I was Summer as she died and then Kayla, they were definitely both on something."

Max shrugged. "I'm working on it. It could be something that doesn't show up in toxicology. Kayla's autopsy won't be back for weeks, so we have to wait for her confirmation."

Something not in a blood test. It rang familiar, but his nearness prevented her recollection. She listened to the house to clear her head. It felt strange and empty with their voices echoing in the hollowness. Raleigh remembered how Aunt Clarice's voice had bounced around the rooms, her Virginia Slim cigarettes smoldering in an ashtray, and Cole Porter's jazz music vibrating through the walls. Raleigh had never known any house to feel more like a home. She'd loved it then.

Could she create that again in the abandoned shell?

Max gazed down at her. "What are we doing here?"

"My grandparents offered to let me buy the house. I'm going to live here."

"So you've decided to stay?"

Raleigh nodded. Her heart swelled. This was where a chorus should break out in song and balloons should rain from the ceiling. She'd made her first decision in eight months since she'd driven out of Texas in the middle of the night.

This must be what pride felt like. Like a tinge of nausea. No wonder she didn't do it often.

He grabbed her, his hands were rough, but she only had a moment to register it before her body was absorbed by his. Electricity shot through her as his lips found hers, heat and passion stinging her lips, warming every inch of her.

Twenty-Two

The ache in her upper back alerted her that something was wrong. As she slowly gained consciousness from deep sleep, the sunlight pouring into the window seeped into her closed eyelids. She squinted her eyes closed against the intrusive light, feeling disoriented. What had happened to her comfortable down mattress that cradled her as she slept?

It was hot though, and her chest felt compressed by too many blankets. Couldn't be. She had her favorite light quilt on the bed.

Realization singed through her. It was Max's arm slung over her. They were on the sleeping bag. Crap. Crap. Crap.

They'd fallen asleep. The night rushed through her. Chinese food. An old bottle of wine from the cabinet. Plenty of conversation, and um... nonverbal communication.

What would Me'Maw think? Her temperature rose at the thought of spitting out any of those words to Paw. If she ever hoped to have a relationship, this house had just proved its purpose. Staying out caused embarrassment if you had to explain it to your aging grandparents.

Max's eyes opened as she sat up. He rubbed his hand over his eyes, squinting against the sunlight. "What time is it?"

"I don't know." Raleigh's voice squeaked. She told herself she was a twenty-nine year old woman, which kind of meant she was a grown up by default. It wasn't as if it were a crime to stay out all night with your... boyfriend. Hadn't he used the word last night, at least once? If he'd used it, then it was okay for her to at least say it in her head. But her grandparents expected her to wake up in their house whether he was her boyfriend at twenty-nine or forty.

Sensing her anxiety, Max lifted her to her feet, and headed to the door. They wasted no time walking the several hundred feet toward Me'Maw's house. She felt like a fifteen year old who'd broken curfew, which was ridiculous. But it was her grandparents. They'd been married at seventeen. Staying out all night with a maybe boyfriend was beyond their realm of understanding. Raleigh peeked around at the dark windows of their neighbors' homes. She hoped none of the neighbors had witnessed their morning walk, but they were probably all peeking out their windows. She wondered how they'd work that into their phone calls to Me'Maw.

They halted at Max's car parked in Me'Maw's front yard, and he pulled her into an embrace that made her dizzy. The anxiety of the morning slipped from her as she heated from his touch.

He squeezed her into the bear hug. "I'll be by later after work."

Raleigh grinned. "Can't wait."

She waited until he'd pulled out the driveway before going inside through the unlocked screen door off the back porch. That meant she wasn't the first to wake.

Madison's chair faced the back door, a sign that she had moved it to have optimal view of the door. A yellow coffee mug was in her hands, and she hadn't even dressed for work yet. Denise did not permit velvet tracksuits at the office. Madison had waited for her.

"Don't worry," Madison smiled. A wild light danced in her eyes. "I let Me'Maw know where you were so she didn't worry."

After the initial heart palpitation, anger surged through her. "I was checking out my new home. Did you tell her that, too?"

The smile dropped into a grimace. "Why do you want to live here? Everyone thinks you're a freak."

"And your reputation is spotless?" Raleigh asked. "Did

you know that Summer's death wasn't accidental? Why do all the people you go into business with end up dead?"

She knew it was a mistake as soon as she asked. Sure, the thought had gone through her mind a hundred times or so last night. She'd even mentioned it to Max as they'd discussed the case and all the things she hadn't told him in the last week. But Madison was like an old antique car that you handled with white gloves.

"Oh, you figured it out." Madison's eyes flashed as she stood. "Must be odd for you, having a murderer as a sister."

She set the mug on the table and hurried out the screen door, allowing it to creak and snap behind her.

Raleigh counted to ten, hoping that would help the feeling of brokenness inside. Had they finally reached the point where you couldn't go back to being nice? She'd accused her sister of murder out loud. She reached ten and felt as though she was going to vomit.

To hell with her resolve. She reached in the drawer and yanked out another Twix. She'd failed miserably at going off chocolate the last week. She supposed addictions shouldn't be dealt with during crisis.

Me'Maw's slippers squeaked into the kitchen. "Good morning. Did you and Madison make amends?"

Raleigh shook her head. Hell had not frozen over yet for a Louisiana winter. "I'm sorry I stayed out all night."

Me'Maw waved her arm as she began pulling her pot from the cabinet. "No need to apologize. You are a grown woman."

Raleigh exhaled. That's what she'd tried to tell herself. It sounded so much better coming from Me'Maw. "I've decided to take the house."

Me'Maw smiled, looking away from her pot to Raleigh. "Oh, Sunshine, that makes me so happy."

Raleigh smiled. Maybe the day would get better. Not

that it could get much worse. "I want to have the papers fixed so that it's in my name. I don't want you'll responsible in case something would happen."

"We aren't worried about you dear," Me'Maw said, pulling a cutting board out. "But if that's what you want."

She wasn't at all sure she could afford it, but she would never allow them the burden of being responsible. Besides, she didn't want Uncle Camille taking this away from her as part of his inheritance one day. She'd avoided telling Me'Maw about his choosing to train someone else as traiteur, but she'd have to tell her at some point. Raleigh wasn't up to date on inheritance laws, but she'd rather fix it now than learn about them later. She couldn't control traiteur training, but this she could.

Still in disbelief at how easy she'd gotten off, she showered and dressed for work. Her mind now clear of the guilty conscience, she ran through all her questions about Summer's mysterious death. How could it not have been a drug overdose? Winter had been the only one to protest Summer's reputation for drug use, and Winter's credibility had been marred by her own recent drug use. The ramshackled look of Summer's apartment had lingered for Raleigh even more so than her crumpled body on the bathroom floor. From the looks of the place, it was as if she'd stumbled through the area, knocking everything over as she'd walked toward the sea blue bathroom at the end of the hall. But now, she had to wonder, had Summer done that or someone else who'd been there.

Raleigh had stepped into her last moments and in her blurred state, had stumbled down the hall. Her feet wouldn't listen, her racing heart, her mouth dry unable to squeak out a plea for help.

She'd been happy though. Even giddy. The kind of happy that comes after a half dozen drinks.

Not the confusion that she'd felt as she stepped into Kayla's last moments. But were the two connected? Murder didn't happen every day in Barbeaux.

Her mind dwelled on it all the way up until when the slashed tire on her driver's side slammed into the lead story.

She cursed. "You've got to be kidding me." She scanned the area to immediately enlist suspects.

Her chest constricted as her suspicions zoned in on Madison. It may make her a terrible sister, but the girl was crazier than a whole nest of wasps. Raleigh couldn't fathom where all the hate had come from, but she seemed hurt that Raleigh existed at this point.

She needed to get to work despite the revenge on her tire. She glanced up the street, wishing Max had waited. The blue pickup in Uncle Camille's driveway caught her attention. Glenn leaned out the window, staring at her. The old fear stirred inside, but anger and frustration bubbled up, drowning the fear.

He floored it and skidded in the grass as he took off toward the front of the street.

She may have accused Madison too early. How long had he been parked there? Had he seen her and Max this morning? That might make him angry enough to take it out on her car. She hadn't noticed the truck on their walk this morning though. But she had been anxious so maybe she'd missed it.

Speculation wasn't getting her anywhere and it certainly wouldn't drive her to work.

She dialed Mike then Max in her attempts for transportation. Both were in meetings and had asked not to be bothered. Even for her she'd asked sweetly? Not for anyone. How rude.

She headed around back to Paw. He stood looking out over his garden as if he were the scarecrow, keeping watch and frightening anything dangerous away. Maybe she needed to park her car in his garden.

As she studied Paw's strong presence protecting his territory, the idea occurred to her that every man in her life had large shoes to fill as long as Paw served as her idea of security. She sighed and thought it best to dwell on that later. Maybe never.

"Paw, can I borrow the truck?" She asked, brushing against his elbow. "I have a flat tire."

Paw looked the few inches to the top of her head. "Sorry, Raleigh Lynn. Your dad's truck didn't start this morning, so he borrowed it already."

Rotten luck. Raleigh frowned. What were the odds? Okay, she may be too paranoid. "I'll figure something out."

Paw rubbed the two-day-stubble on his chin. "Maybe Joey's around to take a look at it."

"Oh, I don't want to bother him," Raleigh said, tracing the indentions of the scar on her wrist. "I'll get Mike to help me out."

She wouldn't worry Paw over it. Mike would answer her call... eventually. Maybe she'd have some other brilliant idea in the meantime.

She left Paw leaning on his hoe at the front of his garden rows and returned to the front yard parking space.

How difficult could it be to change a tire? It wasn't as if it were catching an alligator that wandered into your front yard. Maybe she could figure it out. She did surprise herself sometimes.

She was looking in her trunk at the spare tire when an unfamiliar silver pick up truck pulled into the front driveway. Raleigh straightened up so that its inhabitant wouldn't have a view of her backside when Vince stuck his head out the rolled down window.

"Car problems?" He asked, lowering the volume of the

rock music blaring from his speakers.

Raleigh stepped between his truck and her car. "Flat tire."

Vince scanned the area. "I was looking for Madison."

Madison's car was missing from her parent's front yard where she typically parked. "Sorry, she must have left already."

Vince shrugged. "I'm sure I'll catch her later. Do you need a ride somewhere?"

Ah, but the whole stranger danger message from childhood had stuck well into adulthood. Did she know him well enough? He'd come off as a decent guy, and he did know Madison. Of course, that didn't mean much, and his connection to Glenn spoke even less for him. The guy's references were horrible, but she did need to get to work and he'd offered. The walk to his truck was torture as she went back and forth.

Work was only ten minutes away. What could happen in ten minutes?

And as soon as she thought it, every horrible situation that had appeared in headlines ran through her mind. This was one of those decisions you always read about and wondered why the hell would the victim have considered it. And they'd probably needed to get to work.

She slid into the truck. Even though nothing was unusual about the insides, it felt odd. Unfamiliar. As if she'd never ridden in the bucket seat of a large truck before. She fired off a quick text to Mike that she'd found a ride with Vince. So at least if she turned up dead, someone would know whom she was with.

Boy, her morning had taken a grim turn.

As he chattered about the weather and hunting season, Raleigh tried to stay focused, but she had noticed a hunting knife on the dash board and his words mingled with her thoughts at the craziness of getting a ride from a stranger. She'd been trying so hard too. Trying not to do stupid things, that is.

As he chattered on, driving straight to the Delecroix building, Raleigh began to relax. As they crossed the bridge that led straight to her building, she thought how ironic it would be if her own paranoia killed her before her phobia of the muddy water.

"I was hoping you'd have a cup of coffee with me after work."

Raleigh focused on him. "I don't think that's a good idea..."

"I was just curious about your ability to connect to the dying." He looked her way, with a deep sorrowful expression. "You know I lost my dad last year."

"Oh, I'm so sorry." Raleigh muttered. She squirmed, uncomfortable in the seat. She'd been afraid that this would happen when word got out.

"It's just coffee. I can give you a ride after work, and we can have a cup of coffee."

She didn't want to—at all. But she felt guilty for having him bring her to work and then flat out refusing. What harm could coffee do? Better not to think about it. She'd spent ten minutes considering all those possibilities. She didn't need to recap.

"I get off at five," Raleigh frowned. "I'll see if I feel like coffee then."

Vince nodded. "I'll take it."

She needed to check into a class that taught you how to say no nicely. She was in dire need.

A minute later, not dead and with no chance of making headlines, she dumped her purse onto her cubicle desk and went in search of Mike.

Twenty Three

She found Mike and Jeff in the advertising department hunched over a computer. The advertising department was the busiest office in the complex as it handled the advertising for the radio station, television station, and newspaper. In a larger town that would have been ridiculous, but in their small town, it was just enough work for it to actually keep the staff of five busy.

"Thank goodness," Jeff said as he spotted her. "Don't you know how to place the advertisements?"

Raleigh nodded. "I thought we were going to hire someone?"

"No one wants to work for the pennies they are willing to pay... and sales went and oversold our space again."

Raleigh sat down at the computer. "Maybe get an intern from the university. Otherwise, we will keep having to do this and stories won't get done."

Jeff nodded as he bounced around. "I know, I know. I'll look into it."

Raleigh worked for the next few hours rearranging advertisements and squeezing everything onto the issue. Mike bounced in and out running story changes by her, and between the two of them, they managed to finish by lunchtime. Though Jeff had shut himself into his office after a call from his wife, they disturbed him and let him know anyway. He'd waved them away and continued to stare at the wall behind a filing cabinet. Raleigh took his brooding silence to mean that the counseling wasn't going well.

She and Mike decided to pick up a quick bite at the nearest diner, so that they could have one of their famous brainstorming sessions. These sessions usually involved wild theories followed by grounded rationalization. Sometimes it wasn't as balanced as they liked when the facts were few.

Today they hoped to come up with some theory that would encompass Kayla's and Summer's death. Murder didn't happen in Barbeaux Bayou. At least not often anyway. There had to be a connection between the two.

While sitting at her desk with a taco in her right hand, her left arm began to tingle. It felt as if it had gone to sleep, but only a moment ago it had been scribbling arrows on her notepad.

Within moments, the numbness had traveled completely through the left side of her body. Something was wrong. As she dwelled on waiting it out or calling for help, she thought about how she'd never know if she were ill or being contacted by the dead. It all felt the same.

She studied her chicken taco panic creeping in with her indecision when spots popped before her eyes, bursting into bubbles and leaving her in darkness. Ms. Margaret's thick voice spoke to her from a hollow tunnel of light.

She was gone as suddenly as she'd come, and Raleigh was back staring at her taco once again.

Raleigh shuddered and dropped the taco. Her appetite had left her. She picked up her desk phone and dialed Me'Maw.

"Me'Maw." Raleigh swallowed, feeling her taco in her throat. "I felt Ms. Margaret die. She said something about telling her son that the money is in the community coffee can above the stove."

Raleigh poked at her taco as the silence went on, but after what felt like eternity, Me'Maw's strong voice came through the receiver. "I will let him know. I'll give him a moment, of course. I'm sure he'll appreciate the message."

Remembering his words at the hospital, Raleigh didn't think so. He seemed the type to want an earthly-plane phone conversation versus the kind she offered. Maybe Me'Maw was right: the living weren't all that easy to deal with.

Once she dumped her lunch in the trash bin, it was time to do the brainstorming session. She'd suggested big marker boards for such occasions, but David thought that made their stories too open to the public. She'd disagreed on the grounds that they put the stories into a public newspaper, but it turned out he meant the television station and the radio. David hated being scooped, especially when it happened so often.

Mike leaned back in his chair. "Obviously, the sister and ex-husband could have been involved. That's a twisted little family." He fixated on one spot in the ceiling. He did that when he was thinking and deducing.

"But the ex-husband has nothing to gain from her death, and what would the relationship be with Summer?"

Mike nodded. "That we know about. With her out of the way though, sister could have him back. She could have done it by herself."

"But there was men's cologne." Raleigh rubbed the unevenness of the scar on her wrist. "And men's hands."

"Okay." Mike leaned back, placing his hands behind his head. "So unless she enlisted help, it probably wasn't her."

"The only two official suspects are you and Glenn." Raleigh jotted down cigarette on her note pad after cologne and hands. "We know it's not you."

"When did Glenn get to Barbeaux?" Mike didn't flinch, but she knew he didn't like that he was still under suspicion. He'd been followed several times in the last few days on his way home from work, and it had put him on edge.

"Same day as Kayla's murder. Max mentioned it during a conversation. Which also means that he wasn't here for Summer's death."

Max had specifically told her how they didn't have anything to place Glenn anywhere near the scene of

Kayla's death except for him arriving the same day.

"Well, that makes it all the more suspicious in terms of Kayla."

"Why did he come here?" Raleigh muttered.

Mike's eyes didn't blink. His thoughts were not with her. "Obviously, to get you back."

"But why?" Raleigh asked, jotting why down under her cryptic list. Unlike Mike's neat detached lists, Raleigh's notes were a jumble of words that made no sense to any logical person. Sometimes even she had difficulty deciphering the random thoughts jotted down. "He cheated on me for half of our relationship. He wasn't afraid to lose me then, and then he shows up in my hometown. I brought him home once when we got engaged. Boy, that was a disaster, but the point is he knows where I live. He hasn't once tried to come there to talk to me, yet he's staying in Barbeaux."

"Hmm." Mike's eyes dropped from the ceiling to her. "That's a good point. For someone who claims to want you back, he hasn't really tried to get you back."

"He's sent flowers but hasn't signed the card. He has to know that sending flowers isn't going to get me running back to him. We'd have to talk at some point."

"Don't forget the candy." Mike grinned. "He may have thought you'd go running back after that."

Raleigh frowned. Glenn had never paid attention to that detail. Flowers were easy. He had the florist on speed dial. He'd say his usual and be done with it. Raleigh wondered if Lydia, his lover, had a usual. Knowing Glenn, probably so. "I'm surprised he knew to send candy. That's not like him."

A foreign expression passed over Mike's naturally boyish face. "Perhaps he didn't send them then. The card wasn't signed?"

"But who else would have?" Mike's response was

interrupted by a page over the intercom, calling for Raleigh and Mike to the front lobby.

Mike shrugged as they headed toward the double doors. She groaned as another bouquet of flowers greeted her on the front desk. She snatched the card from its plastic prongs. Max's name in large swept letters was in the center of the white card.

Her shoulders relaxed as relief worked through the tension that had seized her. Even if it was dying flowers with some chemical agent slowing the decay, at least they weren't from Glenn.

Mike grinned. "Flowers? You're a pretty popular gal these days."

Raleigh grumbled, but she couldn't hide the smile. "I'd rather candy."

Flowers received, but why had both of them been called to get her flowers?

In three seconds, the reason for their call echoed throughout the poorly acoustic lobby.

"If you run that story accusing me of murdering my ex-wife, I will sue you and this entire paper into the ground."

Raleigh turned to watch Skip emerge from the lobby restroom. His bloodshot eyes glared at them as he stumbled forward, and to think happy hour hadn't begun at any of the local joints.

Raleigh stepped forward, drawing him away from the double doors leading into the newsroom. They didn't need a scene that some camera guy in the building caught on tape. She had no intention of making the five o'clock news. The lobby quieted as Ms. Betty paused in her phone call.

"What story are you talking about?"

"Mandy told me that you were putting out a story on how I killed Kayla to be with her."

Mike brushed against her elbow as he came to stand at

her side. "We haven't planned to accuse anyone in a story. Mandy dropped by to talk to Raleigh, but any stories we plan to write weren't discussed."

Mike's temper had a much longer fuse than her own. Probably why they worked together so well. Skip stared at them, his eyes glazed over and dilated; his breathing heavy. "It's slander. I didn't have anything to do with Kayla's death, and you can't print something in that paper of yours without evidence."

"Do you have any idea why Mandy would tell you something like that?" Raleigh kept her voice level. She resisted the urge to yell back at him. But it took effort. Her temper wasn't as under control as Mike's.

"How am I supposed to know?" He huffed his chest up, his breathing more haggard. "She's crazy. The whole damn family is crazy. Who gets her sister's husband drunk at a family reunion, tricks him into taking her out on a pirogue, and then seduces him in the boat? The whole family is like that." He laughed with force, waving his arm around. "My ex-wife put her up to it. Dared her. Said she couldn't do it."

Mike and Raleigh's eyes met. She recognized the old suspicion in his eyes and knew she probably had the same look. This triangle looked worse every time one of them opened their mouths. This family's skeletons didn't live in the closets for sure. They dangled in public with signs around their necks advertising their indiscretions.

"Did you see Kayla before she died?"

He shook his head. "Didn't want to. I'd had enough after the divorce."

Ah, wrong answer. He'd been seen at the bar that day. Why had none of them confessed to seeing her that day? Were they all in on something?

He glared at them, shouted that he'd sue for slander if he had to, and barreled through the front double doors; the door slamming and bouncing several times before closing.

"I say we check into Mandy's alibi. I think I believe him when he says she's crazy." And that wasn't Mandy's interest in Max talking. Raleigh thought the entire family was certifiable crazy at this point.

Mike nodded.

They turned to go back through the doors when the bell clattered someone's entrance. They both turned expecting Skip, but Glenn strolled through instead.

A sharp pain stabbed her through the head. There had to be a cap on how many confrontations a person could have in one day. Those Twix in that brown paper bag sounded good. She should have bought more.

"Raleigh," he said, the smile he had did not reach his cold eyes. Her name sounded forced, too breathless.

Looking at him, she was struck by the idea that she'd never felt sorrow from him. He too appeared to be putting on an act. Maybe it was her biasness.

"Why are you here where I work?" Raleigh asked. Her once over of him derailed at his perfectly manicured fingers. She'd seen fingers similar to that as she'd connected to Kayla and Lydia moments before their death. Was he the killer?

He frowned. " I wanted to talk to you."

Mike squeezed her shoulder and walked through the doors. Spectacular. Abandoned with a possible murderer. How's that for a best friend. Mike had told her in his way that she needed to speak to Glenn. Of course, knowing Mike, he wanted her to ask questions about Kayla's death instead of the past relationship.

She met his eyes. She could do this. She was too old to be a runaway. "It's been over six months. Why now?"

"I miss you." He approached. Everything inside of her tightened. Repulsed. It shot through her. "We should be married right now."

"That's gone. You cheated on me and she turned up dead."

"I know I screwed up. It was the worst mistake of my life."

"Okay, you screwed up." Raleigh's body temperature rose. "It's done. Why are you *here*?"

"I need you..." a groan rumbled through his tight lips, and he twitched. "I need you to believe me. I've never killed anyone. I need you to believe me."

"Why?" Raleigh asked, conscious of Betty's eyes on them. Great. Now everyone in Barbeaux would know about her Texas humiliation.

"Because you need to tell them," he said, a wild look in his eyes. "You need to tell them I didn't do anything. They will believe you."

Selfish to the last. He didn't want her back. Not really. He'd come here so that people would believe his story. If she backed him up, people would believe he was the same old Glenn. Not a murderer.

Why had she ever believed she'd be happily married to him? Her self-confidence must be worse than she thought.

"You know what Glenn?" As she looked at him, she couldn't remember any of the good moments. He'd erased them all. "If you want me to believe you, prove it. Prove to me that you didn't do it."

His face contorted. "How am I supposed to do that?"

"Find the person who did." Raleigh walked through the doors leaving him in the lobby. The nerve. Did he think 'I'm sorry' would bring forgiveness? She wasn't Mother Teresa.

It had worked for him in the past. The detectives had tied up all the loose ends she didn't know were even there. His working late three and four times a week or having dinner with his bosses on a Saturday night had never brought any doubts. She'd trusted him, assumed it was his ambition driving his workaholic nature. That is until the police had spilled the whole sordid tale. They'd wanted a reaction of course, but her initial shock and vehement denial had elicited sympathy from even the most antagonistic investigator.

The last few hours of the day ticked by as slowly as it took to make a tarte-ta-la-bouie pie. As they were filing notes away for the day, Raleigh was called to the front lobby again.

She groaned and a smirk flitted across Mike's lips.

"I'll go with you." He grabbed his bag and cell phone and walked up front with her.

She didn't think she could handle any more surprises today. She had limits, and she'd long reached it. She scanned the lobby quickly and her eyes fell on one of those candy arrangements from the *Artful Sweets* store in Houma. It looked out of place on the bare black counter.

Ms. Betty frowned without looking up. "Isn't someone popular?"

Even the sight of a dozen Twix bars artfully arranged in a basket didn't ease her frustration. Why did the man keep sending her things, expecting what from her? She didn't even know. "Do I have to call all the delivery companies and tell them not to deliver to me anymore?"

Mike chuckled and the sound rang through the lobby. "These are from me. I thought you might need a pick me up today."

"Oh." Raleigh blushed. Was it normal for your best guy friend to send you a gift? Was it a friendly gesture? They'd never bought gifts before. Her head throbbed. She needed a time out. Could one of them send that in a pretty little basket with a decorative bow? "Thanks, I was thinking about a Twix."

Mike nodded. His eyes didn't meet hers. "I figured. Let's

go take care of that tire now."

Raleigh nodded and followed him outside into an already darkening sky. Night came early in December, and soon the holiday season would really begin with the holiday party invites and age-old family traditions.

Vince stood at the entrance, leaning against the front brick wall. Darn. She'd forgotten about him. The last thing she felt like after her day was making small talk.

He grinned, though his eyes flickered over Mike briefly. "Ready for that coffee?"

"Not today, Vince." She tried her best sorrowful expression. She hoped she didn't look as if her grandmother had died. "Mike is bringing me so he can take care of my tire."

Vince's eyes wandered to the Twix basket in her hand, and he frowned. "I can do that if you like. It's no trouble."

Damn. He was going to make this difficult. The whole 'don't take no for an answer' bit had taken hold these days. She preferred when no meant no.

"It's on Mike's way. Besides I can't ask you to do that." She didn't know him. She'd never ask a stranger for that big of a favor. He must be confusing her with Madison. "We can have that talk soon."

He nodded, glancing at the basket one more time. "I'll hold you to it."

Raleigh smiled politely and then followed Mike to his Jeep. Maybe he'd forget. She could hope.

"Someone has a crush," Mike said as he started the engine.

"Me? I don't have a crush." Raleigh looked at him alarmed.

"Vince, silly," Mike grinned. "You're just getting all the attention lately."

Raleigh grumbled some comment about wanting to

feel a little less attention these days, and they moved on to running down the list of suspects. They could dismiss every one of them for some reason or another that seemed to make logical sense, so they got nowhere.

Twenty-Four

Paw's distant slim figure hobbled through the dirt rows stretched out before her. In his evening stroll he drug one leg behind the other from his arthritis. Every night before going in for his bath, he walked through, checking that every inch of dirt was as it should be. As a child her days had been measured by the steps he wore out in the dirt, many with her at his side. He hadn't limped then and she'd only thought she knew what age meant. Raleigh tugged her windbreaker tighter around her middle as she squirmed on the hard steps. Her thoughts were uneasy and dwelled too long on death these days.

She felt death becoming part of her. In the crevices and creases of her self, she could feel it expanding through her. She'd wanted the traiteur training to restore some kind of life and death balance. But it would always be death now that Uncle Camille wouldn't train her.

Mike had left with her tire twenty minutes ago, so she'd sat on the back porch, hoping the chilled air would trigger some kind of reasonable thought in the mess of unanswered questions crowding her head.

Each person- Glenn, Skip, Mandy, and Madison- was a piece of the puzzle, but none of them quite fit. No matter how much she wanted to blame Glenn, something about him as a suspect didn't add up. Why Kayla? Lydia's murder had been plausible as she'd been a threat to his secret life. The police had thrown around a theory of blackmail that had him killing Lydia in desperation. But why Kayla? In the few hours he'd been in Barbeaux he couldn't have formed a bond with her that would lead to murder. Had he acquired a taste for killing? That didn't agree with what she knew about him. Even after her obliviousness to his cheating, she'd been able to put all the clues together after the fact.

She searched through all of their experiences together for some kind of hint that he was some kind of monster, but she couldn't unearth any.

Skip? Mandy? Both crazy as far as she could tell, but each time they spoke, they revealed too much just to retaliate against the other. Raleigh believed if they knew something about the other person, they would have revealed all by now. She wasn't dismissing them yet, but if either of them were guilty, confessions were sure to come soon.

And nothing was ever that simple for Raleigh Cheramie because, of course, the dismissal of the first three suspects left Madison.

Madison had said the two of them were business partners. Her last business partner had ended up dead, and even though Madison hadn't killed Claudia, she'd been involved in her death as well. The fact was, Madison had been with Kayla the night she'd died, and Madison had accepted an envelope from Skip that looked as though it had cash inside. And, she'd asked Raleigh for an alibi.

If the girl wasn't guilty of something, then she would have a hard time convincing anyone otherwise with the way she was acting.

Raleigh's head spun. She couldn't accuse her own sister of murder.

Even if out of the four suspects, she was the one who looked the guiltiest.

And again she was left with no answers. At least not the ones she wanted to admit to.

She needed a distraction. Maybe if her brain stopped dwelling on it, she could have a fresh look later. Max would not be finished work for another hour or so, and Mike could be awhile. Raleigh had no idea how long it took to fix- or had he said buy a new one- tire.

She could think about her new house instead. She'd need to decide when to move. It wouldn't be difficult since all of her things were in boxes.

Wouldn't take long to unpack either. All she had was clothes, books, and a few odds and ends.

She jolted up from her hard seat and was through the screen door before her heart could really pick up the pace.

Me'Maw was rocking in her chair, the smell of gumbo steaming up and warming the chilled old house.

Raleigh shuffled for a flashlight in what Paw called the junk drawer for all the miscellaneous items that found their way into the tight space. "I'm going to go in the attic and see what's left of Aunt Clarice's old furniture."

"Good, Cher," Me'Maw said, a cough rattling through her chest. The cool air had brought on the uneasy sound. "Paw would love to see Clarice's things in the house again."

Paw's happiness would be a bonus. Because what had just caused her heart to beat a little faster was the realization that she did not have one lick of furniture nor the money to furnish an entire house. Paw would say she was up the bayou without a paddle if Madison had emptied the entire house. Her cardboard boxes may have to be put to use as chairs and beds.

She spotted the candy arrangement that Glenn had sent on the kitchen counter. The one from Mike today had been stashed safely in her bedroom out of Mason's reach. She'd thought everyone would feel free to take from this basket, but all dozen candies remained. She swiped the one Twix from its spike. Chocolate was chocolate. And she'd decided to relax. What better way than chocolate.

"When Mike comes back with my tire, let him know I'm there." Raleigh tightened her light jacket around her middle and headed out into the darkening sky. She left her cell on the counter, not feeling like being called to work or having anything else interrupt her mission. Mike knew her well enough to know that it would be hopeless to call for advice on what to do with the tire.

The thirteen houses cast shadows onto the narrow street. Night encroached early on December days, and under its cover, the street appeared abandoned. There was no movement from the neighborhood, not even inside the half-closed curtains. Several homes were wrapped tightly like presents with Christmas lights. Two homes had blinking red lights though a few streaks of daylight still brushed their front lawns.

Raleigh swung the chain link gate open to the front walk, and left it open behind her. Maybe Mike or Max would figure out she was here. Definite long shot, but being open wouldn't hurt anything. Spencer might decide to get off his rug and follow her here. Poor dog. She hadn't seen it move in a week.

Even though the white Acadian appeared abandoned, the grass had been cut for the first time in a long time. It gave the house the appearance of waiting for someone to inhabit its interior. She wondered who'd cut the grass. It certainly hadn't been her, and if Raleigh was into betting, it would be a safe bet to say it wasn't Madison. Paw had probably cut it after she'd agreed to take the house.

Again, the door swung open and Raleigh figured she better look into keys and locks soon. Inside, she checked the downstairs rooms to make sure Madison wasn't sleeping in one of its corners and her search turned up empty. The house had two larger front rooms. Aunt Clarice had used one as a sitting area and one as her bedroom. The back half of the house had a kitchen with a dining area, a rather large walk-in pantry, a half bathroom under the stairs, and a small bedroom the size of a mudroom. Aunt Clarice had used it as a library.

She switched the flashlight on and headed up the stairs that were off of the kitchen. Even the framed post cards that had once lined the walls of the narrow staircase had been removed. What had Madison done with everything? She couldn't imagine Paw allowing her to toss it all. He'd been rather fond of his youngest sister. He'd looked after her their entire lives. At the top of the stairs, the light beam fell upon a light switch, and she flipped it on. She'd remembered there being no lights in the attic.

The light illuminated boxes piled high, crowding the room. Every square inch contained oddly shaped, wrapped items.

Every muscle in her body relaxed. She wouldn't have to sell herself to pay for a bed. From the looks of it, every item of Aunt Clarice's had been stashed up here. She looked around and took in the painted sea green walls and wood floors beneath her feet. The attic remodeling!

Fifteen years ago, Aunt Clarice had finished the attic for a woman who'd moved in to take care of things for her. She'd refused to go in a home when her eyesight had deteriorated to the point of being unable to get around her own house. She'd said she'd do old age as she'd done everything else in life- on her own terms. Thinking back, Raleigh was certain that behind all those boxes and wrapped oddities, a modern bathroom existed behind that pocket door.

Perfect. Excitement took hold. With Aunt Clarice's things and this upstairs area, owning this house felt real. She knew nothing about owning a home, but she wouldn't be sleeping on the floor. Everything else was bound to figure itself out as well.

A rolled up rug lay haphazardly on top of an unmarked cardboard box. She grabbed it and bounced down the steps smiling.

Downstairs, she couldn't remember where this particular blue and brown flower pattern had gone, but then decided she'd put it in front. When she passed the sitting room doorway, Madison sat on the black sofa staring down at an empty beer bottle.

Her excitement dwindled. She'd gone and left the door unlocked. A sure sign she'd been in her hometown long enough to be way too trusting.

"You should be proud." Madison spoke in a low, dejected tone. Raleigh braced herself for the pity routine. "Everyone seems to have forgotten why they hated you."

Raleigh sighed. Pitiful and mean all wrapped into one special package. Madison just hadn't received her academy award yet. "Madison, no one hates you. You just need to give them time to stop talking. Small towns are like that."

"You don't understand. I liked my life just fine," Madison muttered. "I had money and a house. I had whatever man I wanted. Now you've ruined everything. You've even put Mason at risk. Are you going to be happy when I've lost everything, including him? Maybe you'll convince the police that I killed Kayla to have me locked away completely."

"Do you even listen to the things you say?" Raleigh couldn't believe Madison. When would she grow up? "You sold sex and drugs at illegal parties. If you are happy with that, something is wrong with you. And why would you lose Mason?"

"As if you didn't know," Madison grumbled without looking at her.

"I'm guessing Jeffrey Zedeaux is Mason's father and your flimsy lie will now expose the truth."

"You couldn't keep your mouth shut. You have ruined everything."

"No, Madison, you have ruined everything." Her insides

cringed even with her anger. She'd deal with that confirmation later. That was the closest she'd come to a confirmation of her suspicions two months ago. Though she had to admit, she'd purposely not asked because she didn't want to know. The last thing she wanted was a personal connection to Jeffery Zedeaux.

"Ouch," Madison glared at her. "How's that for sympathy?"

"Is that what you want?" Raleigh released a deep breath through her mouth. "Madison, you were basically running your own brothel. That's not the kind of life you should want. Your bad choices are on you, not me. All I've done is come home to save your life. I'd think you'd be more grateful."

"Look at you," Madison's pupils dilated. "Get everybody to believe you aren't a monster, and you become a self-righteous bitch."

"Get over yourself, Madison," Raleigh said exasperated. Raleigh wished she could say Madison acting like this was a recent occurrence. Sadly, Madison had always been spiteful.

Madison stood and walked toward the door. Raleigh waited without saying a word.

At the doorway though, she turned. "I thought you should know that Uncle Camille has decided to train me as traiteur."

"Really?" Raleigh said through gritted teeth.

"Yes, I convinced him I'd be a good choice." A smile rose to her lips slowly. "It wasn't difficult. He said he'd rather train anyone than you."

"You've never been interested in being a traiteur."

Madison shrugged. "Since everything else has been taken from me, I figured I may as well start taking from others."

Raleigh looked at her wordlessly. How could Madison be so vindictive?

Madison tilted her head with a smile and breezed out the door, her steps noticeably lighter.

Raleigh waited a few minutes before moving to be sure Madison was truly gone before going onto the front porch with the rug. She'd think about Madison later. This was supposed to be her time not to think about all the problems that plagued her, not add more to the list.

The last vestiges of sunrays hit the very tips of the roofs. She'd be walking home in the dark. She'd put the flashlight down somewhere, and she couldn't remember where. Raleigh beat the dust from the rug against the porch posts rather enthusiastically. She felt the frustration leaving her with each swing.

The dust engulfed her and she couldn't breathe as she inhaled the particles. Coughing overtook her, causing her eyes to water. Maybe she should figure out a better way to release her frustration. She leaned against the doorframe as her vision clouded.

She strained for a breath of cool fresh night air, but she slipped into Kayla's head before the air could fill her.

She was leaning against the red door of the hotel. It felt coarse beneath her fingertips but cool. Somewhere to her left, someone laughed, obnoxious and continuous. It was jarring enough that some of the haze in her head began to clear. A car honk came from somewhere distant and her heart skipped a beat. Cigarette smoke filled her nose.

A large form with wide shoulders stood before her. She, Kayla didn't feel threatened. She knew him.

She squinted, trying to focus, to see through the haziness and the darkness. She didn't feel as if she were in her own body. She was fading away.

Vince's face emerged from the haziness in sharp detail.

214

The jarring surprise left after a moment when Aunt Clarice's front porch appeared around him. Vince stood before her with a puzzled expression pinched across his forehead.

She stepped back, feeling too close. Though he'd given her personal space even in his concern, she still felt the need to be further away. "What are you doing here?"

"Sorry," he held up coffee cups in each hand. "I brought coffee."

He handed her a white coffee cup. She hesitated a moment, but her southern manners wouldn't allow her to refuse. She recognized the label from Ms. Bee's Coffee Shop. At least she didn't have to suffer through someone's bad coffee. Ms. Bee's was the best place in Barbeaux. Of course, Raleigh preferred her chocolate éclairs.

She took the cup with her free hand and nodded for him to follow her back inside.

She put the rug down near the door after he entered and then sipped the coffee. It was over sugared and weak. She wasn't much of a drinker. She'd never quite grown out of the coffee milk drinker stage as a child. Three-fourths glass of milk and a dollop of coffee. That's how she still liked it. If she sipped slowly, he may leave before she had to drink much.

Vince looked around the empty space. "Moving?"

Raleigh closed the door. "I was carrying things down from the attic."

Vince's wide shoulders filled the hall and made her feel small. "Why don't I help you grab something so I don't feel guilty about interrupting you."

Raleigh weighed her options. Free labor vs. the uneasiness of having a virtual stranger moving about her house. At this point, was he even a stranger?

"Well, I suppose a few boxes won't hurt."

She smiled, hoping that he wasn't some deranged killer.

Death and murder did tend to follow her.

"I hope you like the coffee," Vince motioned to hers and sipped from his cup. "Everyone claims it's the best."

Raleigh sipped, feeling guilty for disliking it. "Everyone does say that these days."

She led him toward the attic stairs, and he had to turn sideways to make it up the narrow stairs. He dutifully carried four boxes down, stopping to sip coffee from the cup he'd set on the sitting room floor. Raleigh carried down a lamp, another rug, a small box labeled breakable, and an oil painting that had hung in Aunt Clarice's bedroom. It was a scene of Paris with its outside bistros and people dressed in early century clothing. Each time he stopped to drink his coffee, she felt the obligation to stop and make small talk with him.

They'd just carried two boxes into the sitting room when he'd paused and looked around. "This is a really nice house for a single lady such as yourself."

Vince grinned and raised his coffee cup. Raleigh sipped again and braced herself against the bitter taste. She felt it sitting in her stomach. Maybe she should melt chocolate and drink it instead.

"So what can I do for you?"

Vince leaned against the sitting room doorframe. "I'm just fascinated with what you do. I mean, I lost my dad, you know. It was a boating accident, and you're just left to wonder. Have you figured out what happened to Kayla?"

Raleigh shook her head. "Did you know her personally?"

"We met a few times." His eyes never left hers. She was beginning to feel uncomfortable under his careful watch. "Madison had her around a few times."

"Madison?"

And there it was again. Madison was all over this, and her morals were wonky which made it plausible that she had killed Kayla and believed she'd been justified. Could her sister really be the killer?

She needed to derail that train of thought. She couldn't accuse her sister of murder no matter how guilty she looked. She focused on Vince instead.

Vince nodded. "Madison has a way of introducing people. She's quite a matchmaker."

Raleigh smiled. Quite. In fact, Madison should just become legitimate and create her own dating service. At least then, she wouldn't face jail time for her matchmaking. But since it was Raleigh's idea, Madison would only dismiss it.

Raleigh tuned back into Vince's one-sided conversation. "Kayla was too wild for me though. I'm looking for someone a little more stable, if you know what I mean."

Raleigh mindlessly sipped more coffee and nodded.

Madison had said that Skip owed her for her services. Had she meant matchmaking services or something else? She'd been business partners with Kayla, so why was she taking money from her ex-husband?

Raleigh's head was swimming.

She looked back at Vince and realized it was her vision that swayed.

She sat up straighter on the arm of the sofa. Was she slipping back into Kayla?   It couldn't be normal that she kept doing that. Usually, it would be one time, at the moment of death. Not this being dragged kicking and screaming over and over again into the last moments.

The front door squeaked, and the house shuddered as it slammed closed.

"I know you're here!" Glenn's voice boomed, advancing closer.

The room's sparseness sharpened as her pulse quickened. What was he doing here in her house?

"Vince, you bastard," Glenn stormed into the room and

stopped inches from Vince's face. "Always the same with you. You can't ever find a woman of your own. Always sniffing around my leftovers."

"Dude, I'm not after your *restant*." Vince raised the hand with his coffee cup. "We're having a friendly conversation."

"Just like you had all those friendly conversations with Lydia?" Glenn sneered. "Yes, she told me about all the late night calls to check on her. Now you've moved onto Raleigh, and she doesn't want you anymore than Lydia did."

Raleigh's vision blurred and her head prickled with light-headedness. Not now. This conversation was too important to miss.

"Lydia wanted my friendship. Especially after you kept jerking her around. You were just worried that she'd actually move onto someone who'd treat her better."

"She didn't want you," Glenn sneered, but he stepped back even though his fist remained clenched into a white ball.

Okay, she was standing right here. If they were going to argue about someone, they could at least have the decency to argue about someone other than the woman he cheated on her with. Not that she wanted to exchange places with the dead woman, but her pride suffered nonetheless.

"Is it so hard to believe?" Vince's own fist clenched. Someone else's pride had suffered, Raleigh thought as she sipped the bad coffee. Blending into the background was working as they bared all.

"In case you haven't noticed, Raleigh has a boyfriend," Glenn spit out the word with such force that spit flew out the side of his lip.

Blackness burst before her like bubbles. Her head swayed, and she knew she'd pushed it off too long.

She was lying on a bed with a single dull light bulb illuminating the shadows. She could feel the coarseness of the comforter beneath her as she stared up at the yellow stain splattered on the ceiling above. She couldn't move her head though, and somewhere in her head she counted down the breaths and knew only four remained.

The thoughts were Kayla's, and Raleigh felt trapped. The lightness she felt in the other's body had been replaced by a heaviness weighing her to Kayla.

A face loomed over her, blocking the light. "Wake up. Open your eyes please. You're okay."

The eyes closed and the shadows faded into darkness. The heart stopped. Raleigh's eyes sprung open and her heart raced and throbbed in her ears. Raleigh stumbled back. She'd been in Kayla when she'd died. She felt strange. Her whole body trembled and her teeth chattered.

Glenn's aggressive stance bared down on her. "Are you okay?"

She took another step back. Her head felt too heavy to hold up, and three Glenn's multiplied before her. She felt the same as she had in Kayla's body, but she now stood in her house. Vince and Glenn's argument had ceased and they now stood gawking at her.

The connection had left. Why did she still feel like she was in Kayla's body?

Paw hobbled into the room, his shotgun slung over his shoulder. "You boys are going to leave my granddaughter alone."

Paw looked from one to the other, and Raleigh stared up at him. The man had a sixth sense. She and Me'Maw may have gifts, but Paw was their protector. The one with the answers.

He waited, clutching his shotgun. Slowly through her fog, clarity snapped down on her

She gasped. "I've been poisoned."

She felt her lips wobble and then her face sagged, as if she had no more control.

"By who?" Paw rushed forward. "By who Raleigh Lynn?"

She'd eaten Glenn's candy and drank Vince's coffee. Which man had poisoned her? She stared into Paw's concerned eyes, but then he wasn't there anymore.

The music blared through the living room. Her hips swayed seductively to its rhythm.

"C'mon Summer," Vince called from the sofa. "It's a high like no other."

Summer paused with her hip jutted out and her boobs pressed forward. She wore a red sequin bra and panties with feather high heels. Raleigh squirmed somewhere inside her head. Even in Summer's body, Raleigh could feel the horror in her own. Summer had spent her nights as a stripper, so vanity wasn't an issue.

"I've given up all that shit," Summer twirled to the seductive Indian music.

"It's all natural," Vince got up and approached. He ran his hand down her naked stomach. "It's just jimson weed. All natural baby. Grown right here on the side the road. Nothing wrong there."

Summer regarded him suspiciously. Her thoughts ran. She had no plans to have sex with him tonight. He wasn't her type. He was fun to entice, get all hot and bothered, and give the brush off until she was bored again. She may one day give in just to keep him begging, after all, every dog needed a bone every now and then to know what he's begging for. But, it didn't have to be tonight

Oh, what the hell. She'd done worse, for less.

Raleigh felt herself slip back into her own jumbled head. Summer's had felt so much clearer. Hers swayed in and out. Her eyes unable to focus.

She smelled Mike's sea breeze aftershave, and Max's deep earthy cologne. Mike and Max hovered over her. She could also feel Paw's presence near. His presence smelled of dirt and tobacco, as well as something distinctly him.

Max's face zoomed in closer. "Who poisoned you?"

Then there was blackness again. Nothing came in the darkness though. She felt surrounded by nothingness. She wasn't supposed to die yet.

Light pierced a tiny hole in the distance, and she had thoughts of a light at the end of the tunnel. Uh-oh. Maybe it was her time.

Mike hovered over her though. She felt the familiar pressure of his hand in hers. Raleigh's mouth felt dry. "Don't leave me."

Mike squeezed her hand. "Who poisoned you?"

"Vvv....Vince." Raleigh swallowed. "Jimson weed."

Blackness descended again.

It felt like an eternity before light made it through the darkness again. The light hurt her eyes. It was pulsating, and it felt like tiny explosions in her head going off.

"Raleigh, you are going to be fine." Madison leaned in closer and Raleigh blinked against the closeness. Madison was smudged at the edges, and her crease on her forehead was deeper. "I'm sorry I didn't tell you about Vince. I hope you don't hold it against me."

Madison inhaled sharply and her frown deepened. "You will be okay though. And I promise I won't be mad at you later. If you aren't mad at me for not telling you about Vince."

A strange hand placed a mask over her mouth, and the air became moist.

A dark blue uniform reached across her and she lost focus again. She slipped so smoothly into unconsciousness that she barely noticed.

Aunt Clarice sat beside her in the sitting room, which was as she remembered it as a child. Down to the magazines tossed in the corner and a Victorian chase lounge across from the antique coffee table. "See child, everything always works out. If it hasn't, then it isn't the end."

Raleigh smiled. Aunt Clarice had always had some saying or quotation at the ready for any situation.

"Has it worked out that I still have a pulse?"

"Oh, a pulse doesn't really indicate life, pretty." Aunt Clarice stood and touched an old hand mirror on the coffee table. "I think you are just starting to have a life. The best is only around the corner."

She chuckled and the mischievous glint in her eyes gave Raleigh the once over.

"Do take care of my house though. I'm rather fond of it ever still."

Laughter bubbled inside Raleigh. She'd gone mad. She was talking to a ghost. Must be the drugs.

She wondered if there was a drug that offered quiet in her head.

Nah. For once, she thought she might be doing all right on her own.

Twenty-Five

Raleigh tossed the empty box onto the stack by the road. It felt surprisingly good to empty boxes. It didn't matter that it was only six versus the million more to go. At least everything she owned was no longer in a cardboard box.

She turned to walk back up the walkway and Glenn approached from her left. His oversized black truck was parked three houses up, and he'd strolled down with his hands in his pockets.

"I came for my apology," he said, stopping a safe distance from her. She could continue walking up the walkway and close the door in his face if she chose. The instinct was there.

"For what?"

"Look," he said, his expression softened some. "I know I did you wrong, but you ruined my life by accusing me of murder."

"No, that was the police who did that." Raleigh regarded him, leery of his intentions. She'd dwelled on that simple fact for the last few days. Lying in the hospital bed after the horrible ordeal of having her stomach pumped to get all signs of the drug out of her system, she'd decided she wouldn't feel guilty. Vince had confessed to all three deaths as well as slashing her tires and spying on her the last week. And Glenn had also done enough to merit her suspicion. No, she was releasing herself from guilt. "I left you for cheating on me, and you made yourself appear guilty in the murder."

"You made me look guilty to everyone. You did."

"Okay, so now everyone will know who really killed her. So you have what you want."

His shoulders slumped. "I'm leaving. Going back to Texas. I hoped you would give me another try, but I don't guess that's possible. Is it?"

"No, it's not," Raleigh said finally. "I've moved on, and you also need to."

She didn't feel any of the old attraction to him, and he'd destroyed any feelings she'd had for him during the months following. He had called and threatened to tell the police that she'd been involved if he went down for Lydia's murder.

She did remember how they'd met though. A happy memory had surfaced while lying in that hospital bed. He'd been questioned during a routine investigation of the money kind. He'd been charming and flirtatious. Paul, the detective she'd worked for, had said that he was the kind to be careful of. She'd thought he'd meant careful to fall for too quick. She hadn't even hesitated when Glenn had asked for her number after she'd picked up a financial record from him.

"Raleigh," Madison called from the front porch. "Max needs to know where you want the chifforobe."

Since the chifforobe had been moved yesterday to its home in Aunt Clarice's old bedroom, Raleigh realized that Madison was offering an out from this conversation.

"I'm coming," Raleigh called. To Glenn she said. "Good-bye Glenn."

Her footsteps felt just a little lighter as she walked down the path toward the waiting Madison.

"I've heard he's leaving," Madison said as she approached. Madison's eyes followed him back to his truck and a frown tugged at the corners of her mouth.

Raleigh nodded. "Hopefully he stays gone."

Madison nodded. "Best idea. Paw may use that shotgun next time."

Raleigh burst out laughing. The image of Paw staring at them with his slung over shotgun would never leave her.

She and Madison had reached a mutual truce. And

even though it was probably temporary, it had allowed for them to have a conversation that didn't involve arguing. Of course, Raleigh had promised to stay out of Madison's life, if she stopped blaming Raleigh. It had been decided that to keep the truce meant not talking about any of it.

Fine for Raleigh. For now, anyway.

Inside, Max and Mike carried boxes toward the front room. Raleigh and Madison followed them in and Madison resumed her perch on Aunt Clarice's blood red settee. The black sofa had been the first thing to be placed by the side of the road, where upon someone had claimed it already. They may not know about the wild parties that sofa had seen, but Raleigh did.

Mike placed his box down by a curio cabinet. "All that's left is the unpacking."

Madison smiled. "Or you can just live out of the boxes and skip all the work. It is what you are used to."

"I think Aunt Clarice would be angry if I left all her things in boxes.

Madison rolled her eyes. "Aunt Eccentric is dead. I don't care if she visited you when you were out of it; she'd still dead. You can do whatever you want now."

Out of everything that happened and the million times she'd been asked to tell it over and over, that was the part people were hung up on. Really? She jumped into a dead person's body on a regular basis these days, but it was so hard to believe that the dead would come and pay her a visit.

Raleigh held to it though. Not that she wanted any more visits from Aunt Clarice. The dead really should stay dead, but she knew what she saw. And, it wouldn't be the first time that the dead had visited her. Catherine had visited her only two months ago, but she'd kept that to herself.

A gentle knock on the door made them all look toward

the entrance as Winter came in bearing a bottle of champagne in one hand and disposable plastic cups in another.

"Just wanted to stop in." Winter smiled. Her face held not a stitch of makeup, and with her hair pulled back into a ponytail, she could almost pass for innocent. Almost. Even in sneakers and jeans, Winter was a vixen that exuded ideas of sex. Her eyes only met Mike's and Max's. Always the seductress.

"You know, to celebrate your new home, and to thank you for figuring out what happened to Summer." This time her eyes remained on Max.

Max nodded and looked at Raleigh. She smiled at him, aware that Winter watched them. "Vince will be charged with Summer's and Kayla's murder here. We've been in touch with Texas so they can handle the charges for Lydia's death there as well."

"I just don't understand how he could have done it." Winter's eyes teared up. Raleigh suspected that it was the first real reaction since she'd walked in the door. "We partied with him all the time."

"He claims it was all accidental. I don't understand how he could have committed the same accident three times. Jimson weed isn't even an illegal drug, but the side effects are deadly in high doses. Typically only teenagers will give it a try."

Madison nodded. "It works like roofies. He wanted to supply it at the parties, but we wouldn't allow it. We'd required a list of effects of all his drugs because he only used herb mixtures, so we were unfamiliar with them."

Max stared at her for a moment and the room grew quiet. Madison looked down at her feet and studied the tip of her brown leather boot.

"Thankfully," Max paused. "He only gave Raleigh a small

amount. He'd figured out that too much brought on death, though he claims that Kayla died from falling and hitting her head before the drugs killed her."

Raleigh shuddered. She still felt sore and queasy from the experience of having to purge the drug from her body. Forgiveness may be necessary with her strict religious upbringing, but she wasn't feeling it. At least not yet. Maybe after the memory of her hospital stay faded.

A tear traveled down Winter's cheek. "I miss her, you know. It's been the two of us since we were thirteen."

Madison looked up at Winter and the two shared a commiserating smile.

Oh, Lord help her if the two of them paired up.

Damn. She'd promised to refrain from judgment. This would prove difficult. Good thing Madison couldn't read her thoughts.

Mike took the bottle of champagne from Winter and disappeared in the direction of the kitchen.

He returned a moment later with the bottle opened. She looked at him puzzled.

"I saw the opener earlier when I opened a box." Mike poured the champagne into the glasses as Winter held them up.

After everyone had a glass, Winter held hers up. "A toast to the ones we have lost."

Madison held hers up. "To new beginnings."

Raleigh smiled at her. "To remembering what we have."

They tipped the plastic cups together soundlessly and sipped the bubbly.

Mike looked around as he sipped again. "I'm officially putting in my application for roommate. My house would fit into the living room."

Max inhaled sharply. He had only sipped from his cup the first round. "I think Raleigh should experience living on her own for awhile. Probably something we all need every now and then."

Raleigh looked from one to the other, not commenting. The two before her couldn't be more opposite if they'd tried. Mike, with his shaggy blonde hair and blue eyes, was tall, lean, and muscular and a good-natured and easygoing guy. Max with his olive complexion and smoky gray eyes, had muscular wide shoulders and was high strung and focused.

They didn't notice her watching them as they were too busy sizing up each other. They didn't regard each other with animosity. More like they were staking their claim.

A month ago, Raleigh would have said the distinction was boyfriend and best friend. But she wasn't so sure anymore. When she was out of it, they'd both been there and she'd felt a tug toward Mike. Her head said it was because of the familiarity, but she couldn't rule out the possibility anymore.

"Any plans yet for that new future Madison?" Raleigh did what she did best, which was change the subject when she got flustered.

It had turned out that Kayla, Skip, and Mandy were all in on Madison's business. All wanting a piece of the action. How creepy was that? Raleigh held that the family was crazy.

Madison laughed. "I have some ideas."

Mike held up his free hand. "Hold on. No more trouble for a while please. I think we all deserve a break."

Didn't they all?

Raleigh looked around the house. Her home. She'd managed okay even with all the trouble that followed her.

All the other problems could be figured out later, including Max and Mike.

ABOUT THE AUTHOR

Jessica Tastet is the author of the Raleigh Cheramie series. Presently, she resides in her hometown editing, writing, and teaching. To learn more see www.jessicatastet.com.

Made in the USA
Coppell, TX
19 April 2022

76782244R00129